Pears and Perils

By Drew Hayes

Acknowledgements

Special thanks to Pam, for supporting me on this even when she loathed one of the characters; to Erin, for putting up with my seemingly endless typos; and to Dr. Winston, for reminding me how to simply not give a fuck at the end of a long day.

I also want to thank my beta readers for all the feedback and assistance. To Eddie MacIntosh, E Ramos E, Bertha Tang, Priscilla Yuen, and Brian Poirer, this wouldn't be the same book without you guys. You all rock out loud.

1.

"Tucker! My office! Now!" Mr. Henderson didn't even bother to make his already thunderous voice seem civil. Everyone within the distance of his shout, which is to say everyone within a forty cubicle range, could guess that whatever Clint Tucker was being called in for, it likely ended with a boot up his ass: likely a boot with a pink slip attached.

Mr. Henderson stood in the door of his office, his impressive bulk nearly blotting out the silver-haired gentleman behind him. Dr. Caruthers (he didn't get a Ph.D. in economics to be called Mr. Caruthers thank-you-very-much) stood silently in the shadow of the larger man, content to represent himself physically rather than vocally. His physical representation was quite excellent at that: a tall, lean figure in a suit that cost more than the car any given person on this floor drove. His face was placid and if one didn't know better, one would have thought him to have a look of kindness. Those who were more informed thought of it as the expression an alligator wears as it drifts through the swamp. It was an expression that conveyed a willingness to wait, but only until there was prey within striking distance.

"Tucker!" Mr. Henderson's voice roared through the office once more.

3

Slowly, as if he were savoring every moment he still had in the fluorescent environment, Clint Tucker rose from his cube and began plodding toward the office. He was slightly taller than most of the employees, with a shock of light brown hair and muddy chocolate eyes. The suit he wore was off the rack, the kind of garment Dr. Caruthers would buy for his butler, only to give himself something to chuckle about. Clint was a curious fellow; he always ambled where others rushed and never seemed to sweat the frequent rumors of layoffs swirling about the office.

"You wanted me, Boss?" Clint asked evenly as he stared at the purple vein bulging in the front of Mr. Henderson's bald head. It swelled and pulsed whenever Mr. Henderson was angry. Once upon a time he'd covered it up with hats and toupees, but over the years Mr. Henderson had come to embrace his vein for the motivational tool it was.

"We need to have a little chat." Mr. Henderson pronounced 'chat' the way mean-spirited judges pronounced maximum sentences.

"Cool." Clint slid past the larger man and took the nearest unoccupied seat in the contemporary office. There was a large oak desk, motivational posters decorating the walls, and it was filled with natural light from a window with a gorgeous view of the city. Mr. Henderson had fought, back-stabbed, and kissed all manner of ass to procure this office. Publicly he'd say his children were his pride and joy. After a few scotches, though, he could be pressed to admit it was this office.

Mr. Henderson shut the door firmly and took his time working around the desk to his high-backed leather chair. He sat with a considerable thump and looked at the young man across from him. Silence hung in the air as the two older men stared down the youthful face in front of them. Clint was barely twenty-four, hardly more than a baby as far as these two business veterans were concerned. He had his whole life ahead of him, or would have if circumstances were different.

"Clint," Mr. Henderson began softly, switching up his vocal tactics to keep the boy on his toes. "We're here to talk about Project Jefferson."

Clint nodded solemnly. He'd been under no illusions that this could be about anything different.

"As you know, the program was supposed to create a centralized system into which people could feed all of their e-mail addresses and then access them from a single point. Now, when you gave us the go ahead to begin beta-testing, we discovered an unfortunate side effect of the system. Would you care to venture what that is?"

"It deletes all of their e-mail?"

"It deletes all of their e-mail!" Mr. Henderson shouted, slamming his fist of the desk before realizing that Clint had actually replied. "Wait… you knew?"

"It seemed like it was a possibility when I looked at the code. But the people at the top wanted us to hit their deadline so I rolled the dice." Clint nodded unapologetically toward Dr. Caruthers. The doctor was head of the Engineering and Development department despite his utter lack of knowledge in anything technical beyond checking stocks on his phone. "When people who are clueless are made into leaders, there are bound to be mistakes."

Dr. Caruthers felt his eyebrows go up in surprise. Who in the hell did this whelp think he was?

"Now see here, young man, I happen to have a doctorate in economics from a very prestigious university-"

"Tell me the difference between Python and Perl. Tell me how long it takes an average programmer to write one hundred lines of code. Tell me what a reasonable deadline for developing software like this is. I know you can't do the last one, you already fucked that up, didn't you?" There was no anger in Clint's voice, no fire being verbally released. He talked calmly, as though he were stating obvious facts like, "The sun is hot" or "Coffee wakes you up."

Dr. Caruthers' mouth opened and closed several times, his mind trying to wrap itself around the insolence that had just been thrust at him. He was accustomed to being on the offense; the idea of one of his grunts speaking to him in such a way confounded his strategies so much that he found himself trapped in a moment of inaction.

Fortunately, Mr. Henderson suffered no such dilemma.

"I will hear no more of this!" Mr. Henderson roared, rising from his desk like the licking fires of hell. "Dr. Caruthers is an outstanding leader who has always valued the opinions of his employees. If you had problems with the deadline, it's your own fault for not coming to me or him with them. The one who made the mistake was you, and we're throwing you on your ass for it. I want you out of my goddamned office in the next five minutes or I'll break out the pepper spray we keep for dealing with protestors!"

"Whatever you say," Clint replied with a shrug. He headed out of the office and paused at his desk only long enough to pick up a pen he'd brought from home. Clint didn't keep any personal items at his desk; it would be a silly practice given his line of work. There were a few consolatory nods from co-workers: had he been around longer they would have stopped him and found a place to meet up to throw a good-bye party. He hadn't been around that long, though. He never was.

Back in the office, Dr. Caruthers at last found his voice. "I cannot believe such an important project was handed over to that impudent little bastard."

Mr. Henderson nodded his agreement. "It was a real disappointment, especially given how outstanding his references were. When he first showed up his letters of recommendation were so glowing I thought they were fake. That's why I kicked the decision up to you."

Dr. Caruthers felt a scathing jab wither on his tongue. He'd nearly forgotten that he'd been the one to approve Clint Tucker's hiring. That complicated things somewhat. He couldn't throw Mr. Henderson to the wolves when it was the Caruthers' name on all the documentation. Well, Tucker had admitted his own folly in front of two witnesses and been summarily discharged. The shareholders would have undoubtedly preferred a scapegoat that was higher on the food chain for this snafu; however, Dr. Caruthers was confident he could work with what he had.

"It's surprising he was able to do so much damage, given that he was just brought on to help the project meet deadline. I mean, he was barely here longer than a week."

"A lot can happen in a week," Mr. Henderson replied.

"So it seems," Dr. Caruthers agreed. "I suppose that will be all today. Get your people busy on a fix for Project Jefferson. I want it by…" Dr. Caruthers hesitated. "Well, how long do you think it will take them to complete?"

Mr. Henderson smiled confidently. "I am positive they can get it done in four weeks."

"Excellent," Dr. Caruthers said. "Have it ready in two."

A young couple walked happily along the stone path, taking in the sights of the island as they adjusted to the tropical heat. Kenowai was a tourist mecca, offering inclusive resorts or secluded getaways, depending on a traveler's preferences. Ahead of the couple, a tan man with dark hair and rippling muscles carried their bags. They hadn't bothered to ask, but the fellow was a native named Mano. He'd worked at this particular hotel for many years and carried the bags of many couples. A few times a year he'd also carried some new bride with panicked regrets into the highest levels of carnal bliss, but that was a dangerous hobby and one best observed only in small amounts. On the whole, he worked here because the owners were nice, the visitors cheerful, and on the rare occasion when he got to work the pool bar, it meant he didn't have to spend the whole afternoon sweating.

They drew close to their building, a several-story complex that looked out of place against Kenowai's unspoiled vegetative scenery. They were nearly to the double doors when Mano held up his hand to stop them. The couple obliged, unsure if there was some additional check-in procedure or quaint island tradition they needed to observe. Instead, they stood still as a cat walked across the path in front of them. It was the color of midnight across its entire body, except for the tail, which had a tip that was gold as sunlight dipped in honey. The cat paid them no mind as it skulked along, its eyes fixed on the world before it.

"Sorry, folks," Mano said with just enough accent to be charming. "Got to give right of way to the King of the Island."

The newlyweds stared at him for a moment, then began laughing at such an adorable concept. They went in and got their room keys while Mano set down their bags and noted what an appreciable bottom the woman possessed. He already had a feeling this was the kind of day that could end in trouble, but Mano had stayed out of trouble for a long time now and that was dangerous, too. Mano was firm in the belief that you had to visit trouble every now and then, like a needy relative, to keep it satiated. If you didn't visit it then it was likely to get lonely and come looking for you.

Outside, the cat came to a dune that overlooked the beach and took a seat. He stared out at the ocean, dreaming of all the fish that flew beneath its waves. The cat's name was Sprinkles, and the reason for that is a story within itself. The humans thought they were joking when they called him King of Kenowai. They didn't know it, but they weren't. Sprinkles was a cat and a king and one thing more, and it was this third part that nagged him as he gazed out from his dune. Something was gathering, some confluence of events that would lead to his island. He wondered what it would be, though the wonder was less of a worry than the natural curiosity inherent to all felines. After all, Sprinkles was sure he could protect his island from any threat.

10

You see, while most cats were certain they were of divine blood, if not outright gods, Sprinkles was an aberrant piece of data in the equation. Oh, he had the same certainty as the others that he was cat, king, and godling, but Sprinkles was different.

Sprinkles was right.

*   *   *

Clint sat in an Irish pub, nursing a beer that was dark as a storm cloud and twice as angry. Normally he would be sitting on a stool at the bar; however, the gentleman soon to be joining him insisted on a booth so they were less visible. If Clint had been pressed, he might have offered up a theory that working to be less visible only made you more interesting to look at. It didn't matter, though: the company policy said that the client was always right. This was less out of a desire to provide excellent customer service and more from the desire to be able to claim blamelessness should the client's preferred meeting method end in discovery. Not that what the company did was illegal, per se: merely frowned upon ethically.

A figure in a raincoat and a hat slid through the door of the pub, keeping its eyes to the floor and moving quickly so as not to draw attention. Of course everyone noticed it, but when they realized it was neither a deranged shooter nor a beautiful woman, attention quickly waned. There was a groan from the booth's boards as the figure settled its sizable heft across from Clint.

"You… are amazing," came a strangled voice from the poorly-concealed face. "You saved my job. My whole department."

"It's what we do," Clint said simply. "I'm glad it worked. Did you pad your schedule this time?"

There was an adamant nodding of the mystery man's head, one shake so vigorous it caused the hat to slip and nearly reveal the purple vein that bulged against the bald head. "I told him four, he gave us two, which is one more than we should need."

"Sounds like things are good then," Clint said. "Just be careful what you authorize for beta-testing in the future. The businesses who lost their e-mails were howling for blood over lost orders and documentation. Even we can only do so much."

"I understand." From within the jacket the figure produced a thin envelope and slid it across the table. "Your severance pay, as specified in your contract. To be honest, I'm surprised they agreed to it when they hired you."

"If your references are fantastic enough, they'll do anything to get you. Speaking of which, I trust we can count on you for a letter of recommendation and an amazing review when you get called?"

"Of course. Your company held up your end, I'll hold up mine."

"I think that's everything then," Clint said simply. "Would you like a beer?"

"No, thank you. I've spent the last month certain I was going to get fired. I'm spending tonight at home, celebrating with the wife."

"Understandable." Clint watched as the large man worked his way free of the booth and hurriedly shuffled out the door. He took another sip of his beer and looked at the check in the envelope. It was all there, of course. Corporations were always fastidious about contract adherence. That was part of what made a position like Clint's possible. His official title was Freelance Consultant for Withersby Positional Solutions Incorporated. They specialized in bringing in employees just before bad news became known to the higher-ups in a company, and then proceeding to take the blame for whatever that particular brand of catastrophe entailed.

To put it simply: Clint Tucker was a professional scapegoat.

2.

The life of a professional scapegoat was not a glamorous one. Most of the people who worked for Withersby Positional Solutions Incorporated did it as a stopgap measure, something to pay the bills while searching for more gainful employment. It's not to say the pay wasn't good, or that the experience of walking into a job with the knowledge you couldn't stay there wasn't freeing in some regards. No, the problem was that continually taking blame for something that truly isn't your fault wears away at a person, each rehearsed tirade shredding a few fibers more of their self-worth. It took a special kind of human to survive such verbal volleys without at least a bit of damage.

Clint Tucker was a special kind of human.

When most people met Clint they thought he was apathetic. This was an understandable conclusion, but an incorrect one. The truth is that Clint was simply Zen. Seeing his upper-class family bend and buckle in the unending cycle of trying to amass more wealth had left a sizable impression on the young Clint. From an early age he noticed the correlation of desire to despair, that the more the people around him got, the more they wanted, and the more miserable they became. So he tried something different.

Clint picked the course of self-denial initially as an experiment, comparing his happiness to those who were indulging around him. The results it yielded were incontrovertible. He still might have grown out of it as he aged if not for an unfortunate event from his eighth birthday, one which made any paths back toward normalcy seem far too thorny and dangerous to travel. By the time he was old enough to read a book containing a bastardized Buddhist quote, the words merely cemented a truth he'd already come to on his own: "Desire is the root of all suffering." Years later, he would study the religion and learn the actual version, but by that point the stones were already cast.

Not that a Zen being was immune from physical need. As Clint pulled his sedan into Golden Acres Assisted Living Community, he clutched a bag of take-out from Camelot Burger, the knight mascot emblazoned across the cheap white paper telling him of all the riches he could win from the Camelot Island Adventure Give Away. Clint barely even noticed the words; his only concern was the juicy double-patty cheeseburger inside. For some reason his hunger always spiked on the day of a job's completion. He wondered if somewhere inside him there was actually a bundle of nerves worried about being fired, driving up his metabolism in response. He thought it more likely that the hunger was a byproduct of being canned before lunchtime and being too busy reporting to home office to eat. The reason was ultimately irrelevant: only the consequence of hunger was a concern. Clint walked carefully through the parking lot and past the central doors.

Golden Acres was a step somewhere between an apartment building and a nursing home. It offered individual suites complete with kitchens and bathrooms, as well as some central lounging areas for the tenants to spend time in. There were nurses on staff to assist with laundry and cleaning, plus a cafeteria where those who didn't feel up to cooking were welcome to eat. The mood and tenor of Golden Acres was far happier than any dreary rest home, if only because the people in it still held some vigor in their bones. All the tenants here were in their twilight years but still capable of functioning by themselves, as long as they had an occasional helping hand. All the tenants except Clint.

Clint had approached the owner nearly two years ago about renting a room, drawn by the atmosphere of peace and community that the members of this particular age bracket generated. At first the owner had been surprised, then skeptical, then suspicious. Clint met all the documented criteria, though: he had the income, he was capable of functioning without major assistance (this was the key rule that separated assisted living communities from nursing homes and was taken quite seriously), and he had no previous history of financial delinquency. The owner had initially scoured the books looking for a rule that placed an age limit on who could take a room; however, he backed down after a consultation with his lawyer made it clear that no rule existed because it was prohibited by law to discriminate against tenants based on age. So the check was cut, a few pieces of furniture were moved, and Golden Acres admitted its first resident that was paying into social security rather than collecting from it.

Nowadays, Clint was a common sight walking the hallways. He greeted each fellow tenant respectfully, inquiring about their grandchildren or latest checkers tournament. There were thankfully few between the young man and his own suite tonight, the late hour having driven most from the lounges and into their beds. They'd be up again before daylight, some making coffee, some smoking their pipes outside, and a few making biscuits that would leave an angel weeping in envy. Clint had to be wary of those biscuits; they threatened to drag his "no desire" policy and his waistline into an inescapable wasteland.

Despite his hunger, Clint did take the time to linger with one resident. Mrs. Adams sat alone in a corner of the lounge, watching a television playing some soap opera in Spanish. When Clint had first arrived she'd been a dynamo, a living tinderbox that engulfed the world around her in the fires of excitement. She had organized pranks on the nurses, once tricked an orderly into taking her knitting circle to a male strip club instead of the crafts show, habitually put together enormous shuffle board tournaments complete with sabotage and trash talking, and generally caused disarray wherever she'd tread. Mrs. Adams had built a pyre for Life instead of trying to get on decent terms with Death like most women her age. She'd welcomed Clint to Golden Acres with open arms and a stick of gum that stained the chewer's mouth.

Now she sat watching the images on the screen flicker by, an occasional nod of comprehension as a familiar character leapt across the screen. Clint reached into his paper bag, producing a fast-food apple pie and setting it on the table in front of her.

"Good evening, Mrs. Adams," Clint said softly.

Mrs. Adams looked at him for a moment, her brows knitting in concentration, then gave a noncommittal nod and turned back to the screen.

"You know it's been a month since she talked."

The voice belonged to Rose, a plump mother of four in her mid-forties and the undisputed queen of the nurses. Rose was notorious for taking zero guff from her patients and keeping employees in line better than an OCD marching band leader. Once upon a time she and Mrs. Adams had been something of arch-nemeses, one an agent of order and the other an emissary of chaos. Those days had slipped away some time ago; all that remained was another patient in her charge, albeit one Rose went out of her way to take special care of. That's the thing about having a nemesis: no matter how strangely the relation is shaped, it is almost always a great friendship at its core.

"I know. She loves the Camelot Burger apple pies, though."

The pie sat untouched, a small trickle of steam wafting up from a corner of crust. If Mrs. Adams could smell or see the calorically-saturated culinary marvel she gave no indication. Her eyes never wavered from the screen.

"You're a nice boy. Tell you what: she's probably just full from dinner. Put it in your refrigerator and try again in the morning." Rose shouldn't encourage him, but he wasn't the only one hoping to see a spark fly out of the former wild woman's eyes.

"Good idea. She preferred... prefers them reheated anyway." Clint put the pastry back in the bag and patted Mrs. Adams on the shoulder. "How long does she have?"

"Until late next week. The man from the review board is coming by then to assess her condition. You know she barely passed last time," Rose said sullenly. Golden Acres was a place for people who could still function. That rule was important, and no matter how much the staff might want to make an occasional exception, they knew it wasn't right to do so. This community wasn't equipped for someone too far gone; there were too many places for tragedy to strike. It wore heavy on Rose's heart to think of this old battle-axe being boxed up and shipped off, but there was nothing to do for it. Age and Death were the inevitable prices of Life.

"Late next week," Clint repeated. He patted the woman again and then went to his suite. His appetite was waning; however, he unwrapped the burger and gulped it down in a few bites anyway. The fries went next, followed by now-flat soda. Clint never understood how soda from fast-food places could blaze with such fierce carbonation that the bubbles leapt from the cup when poured yet be flat as water within the span of mere minutes. He'd once wondered if there was a metaphor in that somewhere, if the moral was that living too intensely burned out one's time faster. If that were true then Clint would likely live forever at this rate.

Clint put the apple pie, carefully encased in a plastic baggie, in the refrigerator for safe keeping. He turned his attention to clean-up and only then noticed the giant blue announcement on the inside of his burger wrapper. He sighed, crumpled it up, and tossed it in the garbage. That taken care of, Clint grabbed a shower and went to bed.

He slept dreamlessly, as usual, awaking some hours later to the scent of coffee that was strong enough to have sobered up Hemingway. Mr. Timmons, four doors down, was the brewer of said coffee, and swore that it was what kept him vibrant and healthy. While the healthy part was likely up for discussion, there was certainly no fighting him on the issue of vibrancy.

Clint was less roused from bed and more yanked out of it by just the scent of those brewing beans. He'd tried a cup of Mr. Timmons' coffee once, an experiment that resulted in three days without sleep. Usually this was the point where Clint would make his own pot of mud, sitting in solitude as the sounds of his community coming alive filled his living room. Today, though, the percolator went untouched. Clint wasn't interested in the world around him just yet; instead he was absorbed in thought. Clint was thinking about how not having desires himself didn't mean others didn't deserve a decent standard of living. He was reflecting on all the kindness that Mrs. Adams had shown him in his first days here, and how much joy she brought into the world of Golden Acres. Mostly Clint was thinking about the difference between a nursing home insurance would pay for and the kind that could be afforded with independent sponsorship.

Clint let out a heavy sigh as he reached into his trash can and pulled out the burger wrapper. It took some doing but he eventually got it flattened out on the table enough to make out all of the fine print. After a few minutes of double-checking, Clint pulled his ancient (read: three years old) cell phone off the counter and punched in a series of numbers.

"Hello, Camelot Burger Contest Hotline? Yeah, my name is Clint Tucker and I wanted to claim a prize from a winning wrapper. Oh, sure, the confirmation number is six, six, five, seven, two, one, three, four, four, and nine. Yes, ma'am. Yes, ma'am, I'm twenty four. That's right, ma'am, it's one of the fifty thousand dollar cash and adventure prizes, whatever the adventure part means. No, ma'am, I'm not married. No, ma'am, I'm not interested in changing that, though I appreciate the offer."

3.

Edward Dillon's black-polished shoes tread silently down the well-lit tile floors of the hallway leading to his office. He was a tall man in his early forties, wearing a suit that even Dr. Caruthers would have found impressive. His company, Camelot Burgers LLC, owned the entire building, but this floor was dedicated to the use of the President and CEO. There were few residents here besides him, only a handful of upper-management personnel and, of course, their secretaries. Most of the corporate employees worked on the floors below, toiling amidst a myriad of cubicles and subpar coffee. There were no three-sided felt walls on this floor, and all the coffees and teas were imported and expensive. Edward liked a bit of separation between himself and the cogs running the machine; he felt it kept his head clearer when hard choices had to be made. He reached his office and found a rarely seen employee, Lawrence Farran, waiting on him.

Edward Dillon's office would have left Mr. Henderson seething in envy. It had twice the square footage of a good downtown apartment and the back wall was made entirely of windows so that one could stand at the edge of the plush carpet and feel they were floating over the city below. The art on the walls was original and costly, the desk made from a rare tree that was illegal to harvest, and the marble in the attached bathroom was imported from various locations in Europe. Edward hadn't come into this office by backstabbing or corporate treachery, either. No, he'd done it the old fashioned way: by being born into money.

Camelot Burgers was turning a hundred years old and it was the most profitable and wide-spread chain of fast food restaurants in the entire world. His grandfather had started the company in the form of a small restaurant in Bedford, Texas, with a grill, a few patties, and a delicious recipe for sauce. Since then it had grown and been passed down through the family, from Edward's grandfather to Edward's father, then to Edward, and one day it would go to… well, Edward preferred not to dwell on that thought. The point was that Camelot Burgers had been around for a long time, and Edward intended to see it stay functioning for many years more. That was why he invested in promotions like the Island Adventure Giveaway.

"I take it there's news?" Edward asked. Lawrence wasn't one to come around without reason. He'd been with the company since before Edward was born, and even as President, he wasn't still entirely clear on what Lawrence did, though he did know Lawrence's official title was "Executive Advisor." So far as he could tell, Lawrence kept the wheels of the machine that was the company greased, smoothing out problems and making sure small troubles never evolved into big ones.

"The last wrapper was found." Lawrence didn't bother elaborating; they'd been waiting nearly a week since the second one was called in from Phoenix, Arizona.

"That's fantastic; we can finally get the shoot moving along. I assume he'll be here in short order?"

"All three will be in conference room A at eight in the morning, sharp."

Edward didn't know why Lawrence bothered saying the word "sharp": his general manner conveyed such a sentiment far more efficiently. No one was entirely sure how old Lawrence Farran was, though to look at him you wouldn't guess a day past sixty. His hair was grey, but it had been that color since Edward was a boy, so who knew what it signified? He wore a few wrinkles around the eyes that added more a sense of distinction than one of frailty. He was still trim and spry, moving with surprising speed when the moment called for it. He kept his clothing neat and pressed, his suits expensive enough to be respectable but not so extravagant as to draw ire. Lawrence was precise, like a surgeon's scalpel, a feature that could be simultaneously desirable and offputting.

"Sounds great; we've had all the logistics set up for weeks now." Edward didn't ask the implied question: he didn't have too. Lawrence didn't swing by to deliver good news; there were couriers and administrative assistants with less job security for that.

"We do have a slight problem. It seems your son showed up last week, offering to help with the promotion."

"Oh dear." Edward loved his child, but it was in the same way the sun loved the earth. There was a distant relationship, and the knowledge that the latter depended on the former; however, the two were so compositionally different that achieving any true sense of mutual understanding was mere fantasy.

"The executives assured him everything was under control. He can be rather relentless, though," Lawrence continued. Edward appreciated the attempt at diplomacy, regardless of how thinly veiled it might be.

"Maybe we can just send him to a different resort in Kenowai and hope he gets confused."

"I doubt it. Despite his demeanor the boy can be rather resourceful at times. I do have thoughts on a possible solution."

Edward felt his shoulders relax a bit. This was why Lawrence had managed to stay with a single company despite economics dips and corporate restructurings. No matter the problem, he was always ready with a fix. "I'm all ears."

"We already have a professional team to film the event; however, it wouldn't hurt to have some footage from a layman's perspective. The 'point of view' style that conveys amateurish camera-working abilities has become a valid cinematographic strategy in recent years."

"I see. So we stick a camera in his hands, tell him to stay out of the shots, and maybe even end up with a few usable seconds of footage," Edward put together. "He feels like he's helping, and doesn't cause too much trouble. Lawrence, you are a lifesaver, my good man."

"I aim to please, sir." Lawrence smiled, which looked less like a friendly gesture and more like a baring of teeth.

"Get everything worked out; we'll deal with our contestants tomorrow. You said eight, right?"

"Sharp." Smile.

"Right. Sharp. Of course." Edward did his very best not look uncomfortable in his opulent office as his underling exited the room. It was akin to trying to hide water stains on the crotch of one's pants; all the shuffling and hand movements only drew more attention to the embarrassment.

*　　　*　　　*

Kenowai was an island in the Atlantic a few hundred miles southeast of the Caribbean. It was renowned for its stifling heat, its breath-taking beaches, its lush vegetation, and for producing a particularly hardy yet delicious breed of pear indigenous to the island. Kenowai also held the distinction of having been conquered by no fewer than twenty countries since it had first been discovered. The longest of these conquests had lasted six days, and that record was held by a particularly stalwart group of Spaniards.

The citizens of Kenowai never resisted their new ruling nation; in fact, it was quite the opposite. When a war party reached land, ready to battle tooth and nail for the right of owning this ultimately strategically-useless island, they were met with open arms and amiable sentiments. The Kenowai people would cheerfully greet these foreigners, insisting upon showing them all the natural wonders of the island. These tours involved a lot of hiking in the sun, a process much more tolerable for the scantily clad natives than for people wearing wool cloth and heavy armor. By the end of the day, everyone was famished, so the people of Kenowai prepared a welcome feast for their new overlords. Because these feasts were a special occasion, the food was heavily flavored using the zago berry, a local delicacy to the natives and an almost supernaturally-potent laxative to those whose stomachs were unaccustomed to it. By the time the foreigners would recover, usually around day three, they would declare that everything was in order and if Kenowai kept saluting the flag there wouldn't be any trouble. Then they would promptly cast sail to get away from the tropical oven of torment as rapidly as possible. It was the privilege of the oldest citizen in Kenowai to take down the flag and place it with the others at a display in the local tavern.

Industrialization had come to Kenowai in bits and pieces as more foreigners showed up with intentions of relaxation rather than exploration. The natives found these new people didn't know what a fish or a pear was really worth, and thus their tourism industry was born. Unlike most island nations, they hadn't allowed corporations to take root in their land; instead, even the most posh resorts were owned by someone who lived on Kenowai. They had plenty of use for the tourists' money, but not their cultures. Kenowai was a place where traditions were observed out of belief instead of habit, where sacred was a word that still held meaning, and where they nodded politely at the suggestions of alternative religions and philosophies while still insisting that this was the freshest fish on the island and it would be folly to pass up such a bargain. Kenowains walked a delicate balance, happy to sell their wares and views but stalwart in a refusal to trade away their gods.

This was part of the reason Sprinkles loved his kingdom so. While the rest of the world's countries were hurriedly casting away their roots and legends, Kenowai dipped theirs in bronze and placed them on the mantle. It was why one could still hear magic in the wind and feel the power of the earth when walking barefoot in the grass. Kenowai was a place with History.

Of course, wherever such an oasis exists, be it cultural or literal, there will always be someone who looks at it and only sees the profit to be made from setting up shop and selling refreshments. In this instance it happened to be a man who wore polished black shoes and had an office that overlooked downtown Dallas.

4.

Clint made the call about the winning wrapper on a Tuesday morning. By Thursday he was sitting in a conference room stocked with sodas, fruit, and a congratulatory banner, waiting on the CEO of Camelot Burgers to grace them with his presence. In the room with Clint was a tall girl a few years younger than him with mocha skin and a set of horn-rimmed glasses. He was vaguely aware that the horn-rim was making a comeback among people who cared far too much about style yet wanted to appear that they didn't. From the way she fidgeted constantly, Clint had a feeling she wasn't one of those people. Usually that kind of Type-A twitching was reserved for people too involved in other things to be bothered with fashion, even ironic fashion. She was pretty, too: a lean face and large eyes emphasized all the more by the fact that her hair was pulled and bound so it could in no way obscure her view.

The other woman in the room was much older; Clint would wager a guess she was late sixties at the youngest. She wore a denim vest over a tan dress and her grey-black hair wafted free of any ties, barrettes, or chemical sculpting agents. Unlike the younger girl, she wore a contented grin, merely moving her eyes about the room as if she was constantly amazed by the world surrounding her. Clint had seen that behavior before, and in Golden Acres it signaled that someone needed their medication reduced. She seemed pleasant enough, though, which was more than he could say for the rest of the room.

There was a pair of men wearing turtlenecks and scarves along with their jeans, wrapped in a whispered conversation with one another that it was clear no one else was invited to join. Another man, closer to the age of the older woman, sat placidly in his tailored suit and watched the room carefully. It was likely an overseeing meant to instill confidence, to make them feel as though they were being looked after. It felt more like a hawk staring a mouse, just daring it run. Clint briefly contemplated what would happen if he made a sudden movement when the old man's eyes were on him. He suspected it would not end well.

Before temptation and curiosity could get the better of him, the doors swung open and two men walked into the room.

"So sorry I'm late, everyone. I was held up, um, ironing out some last minute videography details. My name is Edward Dillon, but you all may feel free to call me Mr. Dillon. I trust you have all introduced yourselves in the downtime?"

Edward was greeted by a brief silence after which the old man in the room, Lawrence, gave a reply.

"I thought it would only be polite to wait for you, sir. That way we only have to do these once."

"Oh, right, right. Well, how about we go around the room and say who we are and where we're from? Since you already know my name, I'll tell you that I'm a Dallas native who is still happy to live here. How about you, young lady?"

The girl in the glasses stood up halfway, like she was getting in starting position for the moment she was allowed to race back to her seat. "My name is April Parrish. I'm from Madison, Wisconsin, and I'm currently in my junior year, majoring in biology."

She dropped herself back down like the chair had done some ancient wrong to her, then sat quietly while her ears turned red as she realized she'd added a category that wasn't required in the introduction. Fortunately, before anyone could point it out, the old woman lifted from her chair and addressed the room.

"I go by Falcon Rainwater, but you all may call me whatever name you wish. I have come here from Phoenix, Arizona, but I am from the Earth itself, as are we all."

No one quite knew what to say to that, so Clint seized the silence to get his introduction over with. "My name is Clint Tucker. I'm from Pensacola, Florida. That's all." Clint was barely back in his seat when the next speaker came forward, though this one was far less shy about his introduction than any of the others had been.

"Sup, bros and girlos? Since we're all gonna be tight, I'll skip the full name and tell y'all to call me Thunder for short."

This came from the young man who had walked in with Edward Dillon. He looked about the same age as Clint, but that and his gender were the only discernible similarities between the two. Thunder had dark, spiked hair with the tips frosted a bleach blonde, his pink polo shirt had the collar starched into a permanent popped position, his plaid shorts were lined with all manner of cargo pockets, and the truly observant people in the room (Lawrence and April) noticed when he walked that there was a beer opener built into the bottom of both of his flip flops. "To sum it up, I'm from the Dee Eff Dub like my pops, I love to party, I'm going to be rocking out on the video camera all trip long, I-"

"I beg your pardon," one of the men in jeans interrupted. "You most certainly will not. My brother Justin and I have been contracted to handle all filming of this promotional video."

"Now, Dustin," the other man said, putting a hand on his brother's shoulder. "I'm certain Mr. Dillon would never think of breaching our contract. You should let him explain."

"Could he also explain why we need camera people to pick up checks? I'm a little confused here," April tossed in.

"Oh goodness, did Lawrence tell you nothing? Fine, we're about done with introductions anyway. First off, there's nothing to worry about, Dustin and Justin; we fully intend to utilize Goodwin Cinema in all the capacities agreed upon and at the already-stipulated rate. My son has graciously volunteered to film using some less-capable equipment to provide a perspective more akin to a point of view. As for why the Goodwins and Thunder are here in the first place, may I assume none of you lucky winners actually read the fine print in depth?"

April and Clint shook their heads. Falcon merely smiled at Mr. Dillon placidly.

"Right. Well, the fifty thousand dollars you'll each receive isn't just a cash prize. It's a payment you'll receive for starring in our latest commercial!" He ended with emphasis, hoping it came off as enthusiasm.

"So, we have to act?" Clint asked.

"Very minimally. Most of what you'll be doing is quite real. You see, to celebrate Camelot Burgers' one-hundred-year anniversary, we're sending you on a real live quest! You'll get an all-expenses-paid trip to the tropical paradise of Kenowai, where you'll take part in an ancient tradition of trying to free the island's imprisoned god. We'll be shooting the whole thing, and once it's put together, we're going to use it as the launching commercial for our newest product: The Island Burger."

"I'm sorry, did you say we're trying to free an imprisoned god?" Clint was reasonably sure his ears had betrayed him.

"It's a local ceremony, no different than hanging stockings under the chimney for Santa," Mr. Dillon assured him.

"It seems disrespectful to exploit a sacred rite just for a commercial," Falcon pointed out.

Mr. Dillon began to look out of his depth, so Lawrence stepped in smoothly.

"No one is required to participate in the commercial if they don't want to. However, since the fifty thousand dollars is payment for services rendered, not an unconditional prize, anyone who elects not to do it will forfeit their money."

"No worries, dudes, it will be awesome. There are waves, sunshine, and tasty grubbins. It is totes worth it," Thunder contributed helpfully.

"Yes, totes," Mr. Dillon agreed.

"Count me in," April said quickly. "I've got grad school coming up after all. That doesn't come cheap."

"I'll do it." Clint was less enthusiastic, but it wasn't as though the new development really changed anything for him. This was the path to the money, pure and simple.

34

"I will join the expedition as well, if only to make sure the indigenous people and their customs are treated with the proper reverence," Falcon said.

"Wonderful! Lawrence will provide you with the paperwork. Once that's all done, your plane leaves this afternoon."

April was, predictably, unsettled by the sudden news. "So soon?"

"We did tell you to pack enough clothing for four days when you were instructed to come here," Mr. Dillon reminded her. "We can't roll out the burger until the commercial is produced, and we can't produce it until you lucky folks take your trip and do the shoot. So tonight you'll be in the air and tomorrow morning we can get that ball rolling!" Mr. Dillon tried the emphasis again, finding it refused to metamorphose into excitement for the room. "Now, I hate to talk and run, but I do have another pressing meeting to attend to."

Mr. Dillon's meeting was going to be his bloodstream meeting some whiskey. Spending the whole morning with Thunder had sapped him of his considerable patience. He'd originally intended to come along on the trip for a little relaxation, but he was beginning to think that might be a job best left to Lawrence. Edward would find his vacation in having the two of them in another country, and it would be a glorious vacation indeed.

5.

Experience is more than just the summation of events catalogued into our life; it is the seasoning that flavors personalities, giving them depth and complexity where otherwise absent. The big events we experience can define how we see ourselves. There are also ones outside the concept of what people think of as big, though, genuine blockbusters, and these rare confluences of circumstances can do something widely considered impossible. They can redefine who we truly are.

Mano's Big Event had come three years prior when surfing out in the waves. He'd gone out farther than he meant to, but caught himself before he drifted far enough that return could prove fatal. As he began paddling back, he became aware of another presence with him in the waves, a presence that cut through the water rather than merely slapping across it like a clumsy human. A presence with a dark fin that crested the top of the sea as it circled Mano and his surfboard.

Mano knew about sharks, of course; he knew that a surfer paddling on their board resembled a tasty seal, and that though humans were not exactly a shark delicacy, they sometimes would, much like a college student buying ten cases of Ramen to have more money for beer, cowboy up and deal with the subpar flavor. Mano knew all of these things in a rational way, but like every other ocean goer, he'd ignored the slim chance of encounter as something that would happen to other people. Now he was coming to very quick realization of the fact that sometimes 'other people' really means 'you'.

He'd faced danger before; this was different. This wasn't danger: it was Death. The only difference is he wore a sandpapery skin instead of a hooded robe and claimed his victim using three rows of tooth-shaped scythes. Mano had always expected that should he ever be faced with certain demise, he would panic, his life would flash before his eyes, his adrenaline would surge, or he would lose control and evacuate his bowels. None of those things happened, though. Mano didn't even feel fear as the killer tightened the circles, drawing closer for the grand finale.

All he felt was peace.

Mano reached into the small backpack that clung tightly to his waterlogged shoulders and pulled out his last beer. He had drunk the others after particularly impressive swells throughout the day and now this lonely can was all that remained. It would be wasteful not to let it join its companions in his stomach. Mano opened it with a loud pop and fizz then took a long draw. It was warm and cheap and had all the stoutness of a five-year old invalid. It tasted perfect.

Mano lifted his drink to the sky, toasting to Iohalo, the god of the ocean, Kodiwandae, the god who watched over Kenowai, and even Felbren, the trickster god who Mano credited with helping on more than a few of his late-night adventures. The shark drew closer, breaking the

37

surface of the water and opening its impressive jaws. This was no great white: it was a hammerhead, which meant the mouth wasn't big enough to take Mano in one go. It would be a piece-by-piece meal. Mano remembered a cartoon he'd watched as a child where a sheepdog and wolf would battle all day, then go out for drinks when the end of work whistle blew. He felt that this was probably the same situation now; the shark bore him no ill will in particular, he was merely a surfer who went too far and the shark was, well, a shark. They were both just doing their jobs. Mano decided to show the shark he understood the only way he could, by sharing his last beer.

Mano lobbed the half-full can into the shark's mouth, never even considering the possibility that he could miss. It landed dead-center, the hammerhead immediately bringing down its bone-crushing jaws and sending the brewski off on the long trek toward its stomach. Mano nodded with approval; he was comfortable with his last minutes. He sat up on his board, closed his eyes, and waited.

After about a minute he tentatively opened one of them and found himself alone. He swung his head in all directions but there were no dark surfaces in the water or fins carving up the waves. Slowly, very slowly, Mano resumed his trip back to shore, doing his absolute best not to look like a seal. He made it to the sand safely, swearing to never tempt fate again, and knowing he now had the internal resolve to make that last about a week. Mano was changed by his experience, though, because he now believed two things he hadn't before. The first was that he was mortal - he could die at any moment – and that is a truth that most people work exceptionally hard never to come face to face with.

The second was one he'd already suspected, it was just now he had proof: sharing a beer can turn anyone into a friend.

*   *   *

Three years later, Mano couldn't stop thinking about that shark as he showed his latest crop of guests to their top floor suites. It wasn't the brothers who put him on edge, or either of the women, or the bored-looking guy with the brown hair, or the one in pink shirt who kept asking where the party was at (though Mano did, in fact, know where the party was at, he didn't feel like he'd ever know again if he shared the location with someone like that). No, those were all one variation or another of tourist Mano had already seen in his time here at the Blessed Pear Tropical Sands Resort and Spa. It was the quiet one who brought back that memory, something in the way he scanned the people and the world around him. Mano had learned his lesson well that day; he would make sure to stock some extra beers in the quiet man's room. Free of charge.

Mano opened the first suite, a two-bedroom one for the women, and set down a pair of suitcases.

39

"Here you are, ladies; you be sure to let Mano know if there is anything you need." Mano flashed his best helper grin. He didn't usually refer to himself in the third person, but for some reason people thought it sounded more authentic for a foreigner to have such a poor concept of pronouns. Mano personally held that sellout son of a bitch Tonto responsible for such an erroneous idea, hamming it up for the Lone Ranger and the millions watching at home. The seed was planted long ago, though, and Mano saw no reason why he couldn't rake in some higher tips from the tree of ignorance that had grown out of it.

"What are these?" April had taken in the whole room in a glance and made a beeline for the welcoming bowl of fruit on the coffee table. She'd picked one of the lumpy, hard-skinned fruits that were featured more prominently among the selection.

"That is a Kenowai Pear," Mano told her.

"You think that's a pear? Dude, we've gots to get you folks a legit farmer's market here, and I mean stat," Thunder declared.

"Different regions have different variations of vegetation," April informed him. "They evolve alternately based on the climate or competing flora, and over time can have features and flavors independent of others in their same classification. Like all the different varieties of tomato."

"The lady has much wisdom," Mano agreed. "Kenowai Pears only grow on the island; they are a blessing from Kodiwandae himself. The skin is tough to resist the animals and block some of our abundant sunshine. You have to cut them open with a knife, but the flavor inside is something I promise you'll never forget." Mano contemplated punctuating his statement with a flirtatious wink, but it seemed like wasted effort on the younger girl. He'd seen her type before: out here to connect with some sentiment of relaxation she'd never really understand. This girl was the kind of person who, if she tried to stop and smell the roses, would end up cutting them, dissecting them, and sorting them into various classifications based on color, scent, and petal composition.

"Pears must be very important to your people, and to share a god's blessing shows such grace and kindness," Falcon complimented.

"Well, the truth is we've just got a whole lot of them, so they get put in nearly everything. The stories say Kodiwandae made the first tree that bore the pears on Kenowai to be very abundant so that others would quickly spring up across the island. He meant to slow them down once enough had taken root, but he was sealed away before he had a chance."

"I'm sure we'd love to hear more of the stories of the island… after the rest of us have been taken to our rooms."

The tone was polite and nearly bordered on friendly, yet the voice left no doubt that this was not a request. Lawrence gave a tight-lipped half-smile when the island boy looked at him, trying to see if it worked better when he didn't show teeth. From the look on the tanned, square face, Lawrence suspected that this too would be a failed strategy.

"Of course, yours is right across the hall, sir."

"Thank you. Ladies, shower up and get on some clothes appropriate for the heat. We meet in the lobby at eight and it is my understanding that this island barely cools, even at night."

April and Falcon nodded then shut the door. Mano dropped off the brothers next, who walked right in and slammed the door without so much as a goodbye, then the two younger men. The quiet one shook his hand and thanked him for his help, while the loud one ran around the room looking out all the windows, despite the fact that the view was largely the same from each, just with a slight shift in perspective.

Last was the older man, a single bedroom that still managed to be the largest suite of the four. It had, initially, been reserved for Mr. Dillon and he'd forgotten that peons don't require such lush accommodations when he'd forced Lawrence to take over.

"You've been very helpful," the man said, slipping a thick wad of bills into Mano's hand. He didn't bother to count them; Mano had been at this long enough to know it was far too much for chatter and bag carrying. "I trust if we need anything else you'll continue being helpful." There it was: the man wanted a local as a runner, a guide, and possibly a procurer of wares not normally available in the legal spectrum of shops.

"You think it up and Mano can make it happen. Just call front desk if you need me; Mano lives on site." Mano would have promised this man the head of Kodiwandae himself at that moment, just to get away safely. If he actually did call for assistance, Mano would evaluate what it entailed before deciding if he would get involved. Preferably that evaluation would take place from a healthy distance.

"I will." It sounded more like a ransom note than a cordial acceptance. The door closed and Mano found himself alone in the hallway.

He wondered if he had enough time to get a case of beer and run out to the ocean. There was a certain shark he wanted to work on his friendship with, because right at this moment, a hammerhead having his back would have made him feel a lot safer.

6.

Thunder was on his fourth beer by the time the appetizers made it to the table. He'd tried one of the signature island drinks the bartenders specialized in, but rejected it because it featured Kenowai Pear juice and evidently, "No disrespecticles, but pears are just yuck and then some." So instead he was hurling pale ales down his throat like he was an alcoholic camel stocking up for a journey across the desert. The Goodwin brothers were sipping on wine, a merlot for Dustin and a chardonnay for Justin, while everyone else enjoyed the regional cocktails. Everyone except Lawrence, that is; he stuck to tap water with a twist of lemon.

The seven of them sat at a table in one of the resort's many restaurants. It featured private bungalows jutting out from the main building so each set of diners felt secluded from the world. The table held eight, so a single chair was left unoccupied. Clint thought it had been a mistake of the wait staff that the silverware for that seat hadn't been cleared away; however, he quickly realized his own mistake when Lawrence rose to greet a slender woman in a blue floral dress who approached their table.

"I would like you all to meet Dr. Kaia Hale," Lawrence said, rotating so everyone could get a view of their dinner guest. She was in her mid-thirties with dark, curly hair and a splattering of freckles across her tan face. In another life she might have been an amateur model, doing car shows and local food ads, but the gods had burdened her with a thirst for knowledge, so instead she had gotten her doctorate in anthropology. "She will be our guide for the ceremony tomorrow."

"It is a pleasure to meet you all," Kaia said graciously.

Thunder leaned over and loudly commented to Clint, "Dude, hells to the yes. Hottie alert."

Clint couldn't really disagree, though he probably would have phrased it a little differently. He also wouldn't have said it loudly enough to cast the whole room into an awkward silence. Fortunately, Falcon had either too little care or decorum to let it impede her own questions.

"Dr. Hale, is it really okay for us to be taking part in this? We do not wish to treat your religion with frivolity."

"Thank you for your concern; however, I assure you there have been many foreigners who have been part of the ceremony before you." Kaia was embellishing on the 'many' part: it was actually a very rare outsider who was given such an honor, but Mr. Dillon hadn't cut her a hefty research grant to make his guests feel ill at ease. "The Offering of Kodiwandae is done by every islander when they come of age, in hopes that they will be the one to finally set him free. So, you see, this isn't a closely-guarded secret or earned rite of passage. It is merely one of the ways we mark adulthood, like a tropical bar mitzvah."

"But the bar mitzvah is a very sacred part of Judaism," Falcon pointed out.

"It was just an analogy. We're somewhat more relaxed around here," Kaia assured her.

"So, iron this one out for me, doc: if your Cody-wand-danny dude is a god then how can he be stuck? I mean, isn't the whole point of being a god that shit like that doesn't happen to you?" Thunder speared a crab cake hors d'oeuvre as he asked his question, then washed it down with the rest of his fourth beer. The staff was already setting down another before his glass hit the table.

Kaia smiled thinly. "Perhaps we should start at the beginning. If you are to understand the meaning behind The Offering of Kodiwandae, you should know the story of how he was sealed there in the first place." Kaia accept a glass of water from a waiter and drained it slowly, letting the cold liquid lubricate her throat that the story might more easily depart it. When it was empty she motioned for another, and then faced the table filled with both eager and indifferent eyes. Satisfied she had at least their passing attention, Kaia began.

Kodiwandae's Folly

Kodiwandae was a fair god; he treated the people of his island to abundant harvests and frequent sunshine. If Kodiwande had one failing, though, it was his love for

Alahai, the goddess of a nearby island. If he had two failings, the first would still be his love. The second would be his friendship with Felbren. Felbren was a trickster god from the biggest island in their cluster of land masses, and he was thoroughly disliked by all other local deities. Kodiwandae had a kind heart however, and he looked past Felbren's failings. Besides, in any close-knit community it's almost impossible to completely freeze someone out.

This story begins after Kodiwandae had finished forming the first of his special pear trees on Kenowai and had gone to Feblren's island, Faldilonda, for a drink and a bit of a brag session. Kodiwandae was kind and good, but he was still a god, and gods are not known for their humility.

Kodiwandae had brought a harvest of his pears, which he mashed in a giant bucket and aged into a particularly scrumptious alcohol. Kodiwandae and Felbren got good and drunk that night, talking and laughing and dropping random blessings on passing mortals. The morning sun found them still in the throes of intoxication, Felbren hurling random boulders into the ocean while Kodiwandae watched peacefully. Iohalo, the ocean god, had banned Felbren from his domain after a particularly cruel prank Felbren played on a species of octopus. Without being able to cross the water, Felbren was stuck on his island, only able to leave on special occasions during which all gods were given free passage or when Iohalo was good and plastered and not paying attention.

"It's not like it wasn't funny," Felbren complained, picking a hunk of rock that it would have taken the villagers ten strong men just to budge. "I mean, come on, he gave them eight arms; he clearly wanted them to multitask. I just made their penises detachable and able to swim. Now they can really get stuff done!" Felbren launched the piece of mountain through the air and grinned with satisfaction as it splashed into the water some miles away.

"He'd probably forgive you if you'd just turn them back," Kodiwandae pointed out.

"Forget it; it's a matter of principle now. Besides, they made the deal."

The octopuses had made the deal, which was why Iohalo couldn't just turn them back himself. When mortals made deals, most were written in sand and easily washed away. Bargains with gods were scorched into mountains. Even other deities couldn't undo an agreement once it was set.

The two drank the last of the pear liquor as the sun rose in the sky, and Kodiwandae commented that the light streaming through the clouds was almost half as beautiful as Alahai's eyes when she was happy. Now, Kodiwandae didn't know it, but Felbren loved Alahai too. While Kodiwandae kept his love secret out of fear it would not be returned, Felbren hid his out of knowledge that Alahai's heart already belonged to another. Still, he was a trickster god, and friend or not, a good opportunity was a good opportunity.

"You should go to the island of Denilale and pluck one of the white flowers from the peak of the high mountain, crescent blossoms I think they are called, as a gift for her," Felbren suggested. "They are said to be a beauty that makes even the stars twist in envy."

"Denilale is Her island," Kodiwandae pointed out. He didn't have to specify who; the tone said it all. There were gods in the world - a particular abundance in some areas more than others - and then there were the Gods, the ones who were attached to forces so primal and intrinsic that they lived in a category all their own.

"She has temples on plenty of islands; I doubt Denilale means much to her in the grand scheme of things."

"She only lets those flowers grow in that one spot. They don't take root anywhere else in the world. What if she gets mad at me for plucking one?"

"Would you be mad at a human for eating one of your new pears? No; you made them for that purpose! Whoever heard of making a flower that wasn't meant to be picked?"

Kodiwandae thought it over and decided his friend had a point. Besides, the alcohol had made him bold, and he truly did want to see the look on Alahai's face when he brought her a crescent blossom. So Kodiwandae grabbed hold of a strong wind and rode his way over to the mountain of Denilale. He'd sobered up a bit by the time he landed, but by this point he'd traveled so far it would almost feel more ridiculous not to follow through.

Kodiwandae searched the mountain for some time, finally coming across a single crescent blossom on a cliff that looked out on all the lands below. It truly was a gorgeous flower: white as the clouds with veins of blue swirling through the petals. The smell was like the first day of Spring and the center seeds seemed to almost sparkle in the sun, their golden shells catching the light and reflecting it with breathtaking luster. Kodiwandae picked up the flower with great care, severing the root like a parent cutting an umbilical cord.

He turned around to take the winds over to Alahai's island, but as soon as he did, he found Her waiting for him. She had many names across many lands, but names didn't really mean much to gods: they were fueled and formed by the shape of the beliefs rather than the terms associated with them. She was known as the respect for the land, the hope for sustenance from the soil, and the faith in balance that the mortals held with the vegetation that surrounded them. She was Nature, all other names meant nothing in the face of that truth.

Inherently taciturn already (winter didn't just happen by itself, after all), Nature wore a look that spelled out quite clearly her unhappiness with what lay before her.

"It is forbidden to pluck my crescent blossoms."

"Forbidden? I thought it was just frowned upon, sort of like an unspoken rule of politeness," Kodiwandae babbled quickly, trying to think of a way to appease her.

"Forbidden. Since I first formed them, none but I are allowed to tear them from the earth."

"Oh, well, it seems that's my mistake, then. How about I put it back, you just reconnect the root, and we both forget this whole thing ever happened?"

"The sin is commited. Punishment must be given. This is my way."

"Punishment?"

"I will cast you into the soul of a slug, cursing it to live for a millennium so you may have adequate time to contemplate your mistake."

"Wait, a slug? I see your side of things, but isn't that a bit harsh? I didn't even know it was forbidden; I just listened to my idiot friend Felbren who said it would impress a girl I like."

"Felbren." Nature's face became frosty and cast in shadow, her version of a frown. "I dislike that god. But he is not the one who has broken my edict."

"Yes, but I didn't even know! Surely there must be another way."

Nature stood silently as the winds danced around the two deities. Kodiwandae fleetingly imagined plucking hold of one and riding it back to his island where he would... be in the exact same position. He was a regional god; Nature was everywhere. There was no escape.

"I have spoken to your island, Kodiwandae. You treat it well, you care for it lovingly. You even gave it new fruit to bear. I offer you a compromise in respect. I will bind you in the tree you have just planted and take possession of your power. Should a worthy being make an offering of sea, stone, and fruit, you may be set free. If you can then convince them to carry you to my temple here and call upon me, I will return your power and your penance will be complete."

"How will anyone know to come free me?"

"I will see that the story is spread."

"And if you have my power and I am sealed away, then who will watch over Kenowai?"

"I will protect the island in your stead."

Kodiwandae thought it over. His followers were devout; it shouldn't take too long for a worthy one to come forward. It certainly would be better than thousands of years in a slug.

"You must protect my island as adamantly as I have. Iohalo must be kept happy so he does not send waves to destroy it."

"That is acceptable."

"Then I agree."

The words had barely left his mouth when he found himself standing on Kenowai, staring out from the hill he'd been on a few short hours ago. He knew if he turned around he would see his pear tree, strong and thick against the island's skyline. He didn't turn around, though; he stared Nature in the eye as she glided forward and seized his chest. She thrust him backward, there was a moment of vertigo and a sense of the world narrowing, and it was over.

"If you would, tell Alahai I have something to talk with her about once I am free," Kodiwandae said, determined to relay a message before his consciousness faded away fully.

"I will tell her. I don't know if she will remember by the time you are freed, though."

"All I need is someone worthy to make the offering."

"Yes, but gods are not known for their willingness to aid one another."

"What? You never said it had to be a god!"

"Oh, Kodiwandae, what else could I have meant by 'worthy'? I will show you one last bit of compassion: they needn't be a full god. Merely of divine blood will suffice."

"But… that's…" Kodiwandae tried to protest more, but his mind was slipping away like a sand sculpture being struck down by the unstoppable rising of the tides.

"That is what we agreed on. The deal is struck, Kodiwandae. What is done cannot be undone."

Nature would have continued, but she could feel that he was gone and she would have only been talking to a tree. While she did enjoy talking to trees, it was time to get back to work.

*   *   *

The dinner plates sat empty, polished clean of the roasted pork that had been served and consumed in silence while Kaia spoke. As her voice petered off, the seven others sat in reverence at the story that had been woven before them.

"Dude," Thunder said, "that sucks some jumbo donkey balls."

In a rare turn of events, Thunder's opinion was shared by many others in the room.

7.

"I'm just saying, that's a whole hot wet mess of bullshit," Thunder insisted. He'd dragged Clint, along with a case of beer and three bottles of wine (Clint was beginning to wonder just where Thunder pulled all this alcohol out of), over to the women's room after dinner under the guise of "team bonding." No amount of insistence that it wasn't necessary, or that they weren't really on a team, or that even if they were it would consist of contest winners not the camera man, would deter Thunder from his course. Even at that, April probably would have refused them entry to their room when they knocked, but Falcon ushered them in and insisted that communication fostered harmony and they would need as much as they could get for tomorrow.

"It's just a story. They're used by cultures to convey morals. This one was obviously that no one is above the laws of nature. For a heavily agricultural community I'm sure it was an important ideal to instill, otherwise people might over-harvest or accidently hurt the food supply," April speculated.

"Nah, they'd just say that. Plus, why have the god get totally handed the dick by his bud? This pear god is a pans, I'd have been all up in Nature's face if she tried to run that on me."

"Perhaps it is unwise to blaspheme the Mother Goddess when we are on an island she specifically watches over," Falcon cautioned.

"Sorry, my bad. I'm just saying it sucks. Dude gets stuck in a tree just 'cause he natural-ones an innuendo check."

Clint turned to Thunder, who was finishing off a beer with his right hand and digging in the box for another with his left. "Wait, what did you say?"

"Nothing, bro, don't worry about it. The part I don't get is what the story meant by divine blood. I mean, aren't you either a rocking god or a sucky mortal? Boom, pick one and move on?"

"Most faiths allow for the idea of beings with both deific and mortal heritage," Falcon corrected.

"Greek mythology in particular practically littered its pantheon with half-breeds," April added. She was working on her third Kenowai Pear and sipping a glass of wine. Despite the superstition surrounding them, April had to admit the fruits were exceptionally delicious.

"So there's peeps with the right stuff out there? Then why not come give a hand?"

"Had you ever heard of Kodiwandae before today?" Clint asked.

"Nopers, like, el zilcho knowledge."

"There you go; maybe the ones who have both the qualifications and the inclination just haven't heard of his plight yet."

"Clint, bro, you just dropped some knowledge on me," Thunder said. "But, just to check, no one here is part-god, right?"

There was an exchange of uncertain glances as they wondered if the strange young man was being serious or trying to set up a joke.

"Not me," April said at last.

"I am equally unblessed," Falcon chipped in.

"Pretty sure I would have noticed," Clint added.

"See, that's what gives me the buggins. If we aren't going to succeed either, then why are we doing this?"

"For your father's commercial." April spoke slowly, as if the words would shatter Thunder's brain were they delivered too quickly.

"Just for a commercial? Well, that sort of seems like a dick move." Thunder took a long drink of his current beer, draining the can halfway, and then gave a shrug. "Fuggit. Who wants to play a round of Ride the Bus?"

It took Thunder a good ten minutes to explain the rules of the drinking game, and another half hour to talk the others into playing. One game turned into three or four, and by the time the beer was all gone, everyone had achieved at least a contented buzz.

Clint helped Thunder back to their room and marveled at his ability to sleep as the man collapsed on the couch, completely separating from the waking world without so much as shedding his flip-flops. Clint poured a glass of water for Thunder and one for himself, then went to his room and took his own journey to slumberville.

*　　　*　　　*

Sleep wouldn't come so easily to Dr. Kaia Hale. After dinner she had indulged in a few cocktails to soothe the nagging in her head before she'd lain down. Unfortunately, all this had served to do was make the thrum of guilt louder. After tossing and turning for a roughly an hour, she admitted defeat and slipped on a light dress and a pair of sandals.

If she were describing the night's weather to a tourist, Kaia would say it was like taking a sweet bath of warmth while being perfectly cooled from breezes off the ocean. If she were talking to a fellow islander, they would both say it was too damn hot. 'Too damn hot' was practically a greeting on Kenowai, all but for around three days in winter when an occasional blessed cold front might sweep through and make the place more bearable. Once, when Kaia was just a child, there had been a day so cold her father had worn pants instead of shorts. She'd thought them witchcraft at the time, but as she grew older she would looked back on that day in an increasingly joyful light. It was a day when she didn't need five baths and two ocean swims to alleviate the soft stink of sweat that seemed ultimately unavoidable.

It was the heat that had driven Kaia from the island under the guise of education. Oh, she'd had the thirst for knowledge, make no mistake of that, but she'd also had the thirst for ice cubes that didn't begin dissolving as soon as they were dropped in a glass. Kaia had dreamed of cold, and boy, had she found it.

She'd gone all the way to New York, her impressive test scores and gentle charm making obtaining a study visa no work at all. And upon arrival what she had found was a blessed chill in the air. Unfortunately, what Kaia hadn't known is that the chill didn't stop there; it crept deep into the people it descended on, working all the way into their bones. Gone were the pleasant greetings and cheerfully ambling lifestyle, gone was the sense of community that she'd accepted as the way of the world since her youth, and gone was the world where locks were only for liquor cabinets so the children wouldn't get into the booze. All she found in the world outside of Kenowai was the cold.

She often wondered if this stark contrast was what had motivated her to study other cultures in the first place, hoping perhaps to find one she loved as dearly as her home but without the insufferable swelter. Instead she'd wound up visiting here more and more frequently, trying to convince herself it was for research on the many myths and legends her island had collected.

Kaia paused as she walked along the dunes. Though her eyes had been set on the ocean, she'd still noticed a waving tip of gold slicing its way through the night ahead of her. She smiled as she stopped and inclined her head. "My King."

The King of Kenowai paid her no heed, but whether that was a side effect of his royal airs or his catly nature one could never really be sure. Kaia had always meant to look into how the strange feline had acquired this title yet she could never seem to remember it when it was time for new projects. The idea was like a cat itself: impossible to trap and seen only when it desired to be.

She watched as the King of Kenowai made his way up a hill that rose from the dunes and jutted out over the ocean, moving toward the top where a local was sitting with a six-pack. Kaia wondered what the King would say of her expedition tomorrow, whether he would chastise Kaia like her mother or quote her father and say she had forgotten her own culture while chasing everyone else's. More than likely it would be none of these things; instead the King of Kenowai would likely just stare at her and swish his strange tail, waiting for her to finish her rambling or give him a fish.

Kaia turned around and headed back toward the resort. The others would sleep later than she. When you lived in a climate this warm, you grew accustomed to getting things done in the first and last parts of the day, so she would use her time in the morning to visit one of the fish merchants out on the pier. She knew it was impossible to bribe someone like the King of Kenowai, but giving him a nice treat would still make her feel better. Perhaps it might even be the trick that finally let her sleep.

*   *   *

Sprinkles climbed the hill that looked over the sea at his own pace, which is to say the perfect one. He arrived as one of his subjects was opening a fresh can of beer. Instead of drinking it like most of the humans tended to do, this one stuck his arm out over the side and let the amber liquid fall down into the ocean, moonlight sparkling through it as it descended. Sprinkles cast the human a curious glance; what meaning was there to this waste of the island's resources?

"Hello there, Your Majesty. I bet you wonder why I'm pouring beer into the water."

Cats are ill-equipped for the rolling of eyes, but Sprinkles somehow conveyed the sentiment all the same.

"I got a friend in the waves who can't get these on his own, so every now and then I come up and pour some for him."

This was acceptable to Sprinkles. Wasting of anything here was frowned upon, but sharing was a whole different matter. Sprinkles moved closer to the human and took a seat mere feet away, a great honor for the lower being. He gazed out at the churning waters, at the sandy, shifting line where his kingdom ended and another's began. It was a strange feeling, looking at a piece of the world that wasn't under his control. It hurt his pride, yet he knew it was important because it humbled him. Sprinkles was a king, not a tyrant, and recognizing those sandy lines was one of the many important distinctions between the two.

"You know, everyone always talks about your tail when they see you. It is attention grabbing, but I don't understand why no one talks about your eyes. How many cats have golden eyes?"

If Sprinkles could have talked, he would have said nothing. If he could have talked and the boy had plied him with just the right combinations of milk, fish, and worship, then Sprinkles might have said "Four." Then again, it had been a long time since Sprinkles had left his kingdom; the number might have changed since he last checked. So perhaps it was better that Sprinkles said nothing.

His silence was a trait that could certainly explain why he was one the few kings to ever be genuinely loved by the entirety of his people.

*   *   *

Many miles away, beneath the tumbling chaos of the waves into the dark peace that dwells deeper, a silent shape cut through the water. It was a machine of perfect destruction, likely crafted by some forgotten god with a grudge against the world and honed by the eternal cockfight that was evolution. It smelled many things in the waters that flowed past: it smelled blood and piss and fear and victory and pain. It smelled entire lives, born and snuffed out in a perfect progression of scents. It smelled death, both the kind that had already come and the kind that was still on its way. Sometimes it thought it even smelled its own death, but it shook off such thoughts as nonsense when they came. It did smell something else in the salty water, though, a rare treat it always enjoyed.

People say that sharks are incapable of smiling because they lack the necessary muscles to manipulate their mouths for such a social purpose. What those people haven't realized is that sharks are, in fact, always smiling. When you are that powerful of a being, there's no reason not to.

Of course, even sharks have waffling levels of delight. As the hammerhead began moving closer to shore, its cheer definitely began to rise. It just hoped the human had poured a darker beer than last time. It was an unstoppable embodiment of killing and eating; there was no way it was going to get a decent buzz off some blonde ale.

8.

The next morning found all of the travelers, except Lawrence, gathered in the hotel lobby. Kaia informed them that she would be walking them through the ceremony, both the gathering of the ingredients and the actual offering, while the Goodwin brothers and Thunder recorded the whole thing. Sprinkles sat by her legs, cleaning his paws, and listened with half-hearted interest. The woman's words meant nothing to him, but she had paid him homage at daybreak with a couple of sizable fish, so he was honoring her with his company for some time before attending to his royal duties.

Proper acknowledgement of fealty aside, there was another reason Sprinkles was hanging out. There was some indescribable feature of this group, a scent that he found intriguing. It was a scent that even the hammerhead wouldn't have picked up on, for while sharks can smell lives and deaths, only those of divine heritage can pick up the perfume of fate.

"The offering has three essential ingredients as we're told by the story: stone, sea, and fruit. Now, the stone is traditionally a perfectly elliptical rock found on the slopes of the Rilletien Hills. The sea is a cup of water from a natural inlet that we locals call Nature's Pool of Tears. The fruit is, of course, a Kenowai Pear plucked from the tree where Kodiwandae has been imprisoned."

"That's it? I thought it would be more complex," April interrupted.

"The ingredients are not the difficult part. It is the worthiness of the ones making the offering that is the true trial," Kaia explained.

"Since I'm forced to suppose that none of us quite fit the bill, what do we do after nothing happens?" Clint asked.

"We wait an appropriate amount of time, then open the pear and cut it into slices, one for each person present. We eat it to show the great goddess of the land that we understand her decision to judge us unworthy and still pay her homage for the bounties she provides us."

"That is beautiful," Falcon said, her eyes going a little misty.

"Yeah, just one snarl in the tangles, though. What if one of us is just all up on not eating pears? I mean, like, avoiding them is a lifestyle thing."

Kaia resisted the urge to roll her eyes and smiled at Thunder. "Then that person may choose not to eat his or her slice. I should mention, though, in our culture such an act is a way to show the goddess that you curse her for calling you unworthy. It would be the equivalent of spitting in her eye."

"Fuck bucket," Thunder swore. "I guess I better hope it works then."

"If we could move this along, some of us are here to create true film and would like to get moving while the light is good," Dustin complained.

Kaia nodded respectfully. "Of course. I've got a vehicle arranged to take us to the Rilletien Hills."

As they piled into the tour bus, emptied of its usual passenger load for today's private chartering, there was much mumbling and discussion of the day's plans. In all the discussion, however, not one person inquired as to why Lawrence had opted not to join them. It wasn't that they didn't care, but rather that they believed some magical spell had been woven over them in the gift of his absence and that speaking his name aloud would shred it like a broom through a cobweb. Names are powerful things, and no one was particularly anxious to invoke Lawrence's presence by using his.

Dr. Kaia Hale was the last passenger in the line, and she was surprised to see the King of Kenowai hop onto the steps alongside her. She stared down at the cat with the curious tail.

"Are you certain? We won't be back for some hours."

Sprinkles bounded ahead of her, past the bus driver (who was about to object to an animal on his vessel until he saw the tip of gold and bowed his head) and down to an empty seat where he hopped up and stared out the window. It didn't matter how long the ride would take; this was interesting now. Besides, his island was not a tremendous one. He could make it anywhere in half a day's journey, so if he grew bored, he would amble through his kingdom.

"So be it," Kaia said more to herself than to anyone else. The King had no need of her permission, and no one else would have really understood what she was talking about. The doors sealed shut behind her as the driver ground the bus's ancient gears and set off down the road.

*   *   *

Lawrence was, it turned out, neither sick nor tired. He had merely done his job well enough that his presence was no longer required. Oh, he'd have to lord over the Goodwins in the editing room, that much was certain, and getting everyone back safe and sound would fall on his shoulders as well, but for today, the dominos were all set in motion and it was time to relax. A good fixer did not create work where there was none and he did not ignore rest time when it was presented.

So Lawrence, intimidating psychological figure that he was, took the day to use the resort's impressive spa facilities. He was massaged, mud-wrapped, steamed, saunaed, and just generally basted with comfort. It was a good chance to get back to zero and let his tension melt away. He was certain the world would seek to refill his cup of stress immediately, but that was okay. That was what the world did, and Lawrence would pour out that stress with skill and vigor, because that was what Lawrence did. Oh sure, occasionally an errant thought would slip through his mind about the chance of something going wrong, but he quickly soothed such insecurities away. Everything had been taken care of; not even Thunder could mess it up. Today, he relaxed. Tomorrow, he resumed his usual cynical outlook.

*   *   *

The trip out to Rilletien Hills had proven to be more time-consuming than expected. It wasn't the getting there that was hard: it was the stone selection process.

The contest winners had immediately disembarked from the bus and begun scouring the area for an acceptable stone while the video crew captured their movements. Kaia was the judge since she was the expert, taking each one and turning it over in her hands, running her fingers delicately along the surface, and ultimately dropping it to her feet when it failed to meet muster. At first they respected her dedication to the importance of selecting an offering worthy of her god, but as the sun grew hotter and the pile of rocks at her feet grew larger, even Falcon began to wonder if she was getting paid per rejection. At last she declared one of Clint's stones, a smaller one that he had found when the cat knocked it down the hill at him, to be adequate, and they were shuffled back into the somewhat-less stifling heat of the bus.

Nature's Pool of Tears was much prettier, a natural inlet surrounded by white sands and lush trees. Kaia told them that during the right season the entire cove would fill with light during a sunset, like it was hoarding it there in case the sun decided not to rise the next day. Of course, at this location, the process was as simple as taking a water bottle from Kaia and filling it up. They didn't even have a chance to swim. It was a little depressing until Thunder reminded them that they had two days left after this, which left plenty of time to come back.

They re-herded onto the bus and departed, though the next drive took some time. Kodiwandae's first tree sat in the center of the island, away from the scenic shores and other areas easily coupled with tourism. The road that took them to it was made of dirt and curves, weaving through trees as it ascended a hill. The driver was constantly mashing the bus's poor gears in an effort to make sure they sacrificed not even a small scrap of momentum. Kaia had discovered in her studies that most cultures required time spent in solemn prayer before any ceremonies of great importance could take place. She often wondered if this road was the gods' way of ensuring that anyone who tried to make the offering engaged in the prerequisite of prayer even without supervision. If so, she had to admit it was an effective strategy.

At last the road leveled off and they broke into a relatively small clearing. It was surrounded by various flora on all sides, but clear in the center except for a massive pear tree jutting from the ground. Though it was gnarled and old, countless Kenowai Pears hung from its branches, each seeming more ripe and luscious than the last.

There was oohing and aahing at its majesty until the Goodwins swooped in and began ordering everyone into positions. The driver was forced, despite ample protest, to move his bus back down the road a bit so it wouldn't accidentally end up in any shots. Thunder was physically dragged away from the others and Kaia stood directly behind Justin as he set up his camera so as not to get in the way.

"Wait, we've got the cat in the shot," Dustin called from a few feet away. "Somebody toss him out."

Kaia felt her blood race at such disrespect. As her face flushed, she turned on her heel, ready to deliver a violent tongue-lashing at the rude camera man. Luckily for most involved, Clint beat her to the punch.

"The cat's been in every other shot so far. Why not just leave it be?"

Dustin looked over at his brother. "Is that true? I don't remember seeing it in any."

"No, bro, Clint is smash on the money. It was jumping wimbly-style on the rocks and was dropping a paw in the water trying to get some fish when we filled the bottle," Thunder answered.

Justin shrugged. "I wasn't paying attention to the local animals; I thought it would all blend in to the background."

"Damn it. Fine; leave the cat in, but somebody hold him so he doesn't go scampering around and ruin the shot."

Clint reached down and picked up the King of Kenowai before anyone, especially the King, had a chance to object. "Sorry, little guy, I know cats aren't big on being held but it will make everything run smoother."

"So, we've got all the stuff, what do we do now?" April asked, holding up the bottle and rock she'd been tasked with carrying.

"When the Goodwins tell you to start, you will go to the small altar set up in front of the tree. Pour the water into the depression on the top then drop in the stone. After that, you pluck a pear from the tree and set it on the stone. The density of the objects works in such a way that the pear should balance perfectly, the water holding it in place. When all that is done, you tell the goddess that the offering is assembled and you wished to be judged for the right of freeing Kodiwandae," Kaia explained.

"Sounds simple enough," April mumbled under her breath. Falcon was staring wide-eyed at the natural beauty surrounding them and Clint was holding the cat, so it fell to her to do the manual work.

"We're good here," Justin called out.

"Ditto. You can begin whenever you're ready," Dustin agreed.

"Totes rocking over here," Thunder added.

Kaia watched from her place on the sidelines as the dark-skinned girl began setting up the offering just as instructed. She had an impressive eye for detail, this one; many of the worshippers Kaia had overseen were quick with it, wanting to be done and on to the next part. Not this girl; she was meticulous, pouring the water like it was going into her thirsty lover's mouth and setting the stone in the exact center so as to make the balancing possible. She showed equal care in selection of the pear, touching many, thumping a few, and then finally plucking one nearly on the opposite side of the tree. She placed it down gently, and just as promised, it didn't so much as wobble.

"I guess we're ready," April said, motioning the others closer. Falcon, Clint, and Sprinkles all joined her in surrounding the altar.

"May I?" Falcon asked respectfully.

"Fine with me," Clint said.

"At least you believe in this stuff," April agreed.

"Many thanks to you both." Falcon turned her attention to the pear and the tree then lifted her eyes to the heavens. "Oh Mighty Goddess from whom all earth springs. We mortals beg you hear our prayers and observe this offering to you. We have come humbly to beseech you to free the trapped god, Kodiwandae, so that he might return to his island and the worshippers who need him."

"Are you getting any feedback?" Justin whispered over the two-way headsets he and Dustin wore when shooting.

"Yeah, a bit of a weird high-pitched tremble. I'm trying to compensate for it," Dustin replied.

Kaia heard something, too: a soft crackle that seemed to be coming from everywhere at once. Also, she couldn't be a hundred percent certain, but she was pretty sure the sky had been clear a minute ago, not thick with grey puffy clouds as it was now.

"Though we know we are but mere humans, we ask this of you, Great Goddess. To show you respect, we have done as you asked and brought offerings of stone, sea, and fruit. Please, Goddess, if any of those assembled be worthy, we humbly beg you to free Kodiwandae."

"Cut!" Dustin yelled standing from his camera. He had to yell because the wind, which had been gentle and tropical moments before, was howling around them and whipping through the tree's branches. "We've got to try again; the feedback on these things is getting unworkable."

The crackle was audible now, not just a soft background noise but a piercing note that penetrated even the wind. As Kaia watched, she could swear she saw occasional golden bolts flashing between the limbs of the tree. Somewhere, somewhere deep down under all her essays and studies and term papers, somewhere that Kaia hadn't trusted since she was little girl, a creeping sensation of what was occurring began to gnaw at her.

Falcon paid Dustin no mind, continuing to yell up at the sky to be heard over the wind. "Great Goddess, we beseech you on bended knee, please deem one of us worthy. Please set this god free!"

"Guys… I don't think we're going to be doing this again," Thunder said, his usual flippant tones absent as he stared as the now-undeniable arcs of golden energy leaping from branch to branch. The thrum grew higher and a new sound filled the air, this one like a bubble of grease bursting over a hot griddle.

"Shit!" Justin leapt aside as a shower of sparks spewed forth from his very, very expensive camera. Dustin's followed suit less than ten seconds later, and both brothers sat helpless on the ground as the tools they built their career on fizzled and popped their way into the scrap heap.

"You!" Dustin said, finding his anger and jabbing it, along with his finger, at Kaia. "What the hell is all this? Did you set up some special effects to try and make it more dramatic?"

"It's… impossible," Kaia said, looking for anything from her formerly rock-solid world of facts to cling onto. After much grasping, she succeeded in closing around something. "It's impossible! It must be some freak storm. It can't be the god. Kodiwandae can only be released in the presence of someone with the blood of a god!"

It's funny the way wind works: had Kaia found her fact and voiced it any sooner, the wind would have blown it to the east, away from the ears of those at the altar and leaving us with a very different story. The breeze that grabbed Kaia's words was a northward one, though, and it brought her whole statement to the ears of three nervous humans and one mildly-interested cat.

Cats have not developed the ability to accurately convey a sense of panic, predominantly because such a sensation goes counter to their nature. As it is, their faces are really only suited for expressing displeasure and disdain. Sprinkles was not an ordinary cat, though, and had anyone been paying attention to him instead of the sky, they would have seen a very pronounced "Oh Shit" look on his furry face as he realized what was happening.

"Hey, calm down," Clint said as the cat began struggling to get free of his arms. The golden lightning was arcing closer to the center of the tree now, the trunk beginning to glow with a steadily brightening light. Cats are already experts in freeing themselves, and ones with a bit of divine blood move into the realm of supernatural. For an instant Clint felt like he was trying to keep his grip on a shadow dunked in mercury; then it was over and the cat was racing across the field away from him.

Clint turned to yell after him, and that's why he didn't see the burst of light like everyone else. It ripped from the tree, coursed through the pear, and struck Clint in the dead center of his back, hurling him through the air until he landed several feet away.

Clint's head swirled, his brain trying to make sense of what had just happened. He'd almost puzzled it out when a voice rang through his skull, different from any of the ones he'd heard that day. It sounded young, yet authoritative. Clint couldn't understand the words it spoke, not really, but the sentiment attached was as clear as if it had come from the recesses of Clint's own mind.

Fuck it feels good to be out of there!

Clint, with little pomp or to-do, bid the waking world adieu and passed right the hell out.

9.

Though Clint's attitude of avoiding desire was sprung largely from his observations of his family, there was a catalyst in the form of an event that brought it all together for him. It was an experience he endeavored to forget, though it lived on at the back of his mind and often resurfaced during precarious moments to shape his decisions.

Clint was the youngest of three children, having two older sisters. The eldest was named Charlotte and Clint loved her dearly. She was warm and kind toward him, though somewhat less amiable with the rest of the world. Charlotte saw something decent in her little brother, something she wanted to nurture rather than see it torn away from him, the way the world often does to people with such decency. She would spend time with him, read to him, and even reassure him on particularly scary stormy nights. She did this in spite of her full burden at law school, working hard to make the time to show care for the odd duckling her family had produced. This was all before the time for the bar came.

As her climatic test drew nearer, Charlotte had less and less time to spend with Clint. He missed his sister, and when she did emerge from her cavernous room, she was short and grumpy, angry at the fact that she had to leave her books for any reason, even biological imperatives. With her gone, Clint began to understand just how lonely the world around him was. He was an optimistic boy, though, and as his birthday drew close, he hoped to see even a flash more of the Charlotte he'd known before. Poor Clint didn't realize that his party was the day before her exam.

When the big day came, his friends gathered in the backyard, stuffing themselves with sugary cake and releasing the energy on pointless party games. His parents had even hired a clown to entertain the tykes while the other adults sipped chardonnay and enjoyed the break from their responsibilities. Of course, an entire gaggle of six year olds coupled with blaring party music and the frequent bouts of applause at various clown tricks does not generate an environment conducive to studying.

No one really thought about how loud it was getting until a tall figure with messy hair came striding across the lawn. Charlotte looked less like a future lawyer than she did an academic Valkyrie, a warrior of words and books whose wrath had been foolishly invoked. She stared around the yard, her senses overloading after weeks spent only with scribbled lines and a bright computer screen. She needed to vent, but even in this state she knew better than to turn her ire on the children. The parents were out too, their silent sipping making them improper targets for outrage at the racket. Then a balloon burst to her left, causing the children to clap, and just like that Charlotte had found her target.

Clint watched in mute horror as his sweet, kind, loving older sister walked right up to the clown and delivered a vicious right hook to his temple. The clown staggered back; unfortunately for everyone, Charlotte was not the first irate party guest who had ever taken a swing at him. He got his bearings and let fly with a floppy-shoed kick to her abdomen. Just like that it was a brawl, Charlotte grabbing random party favors as makeshift weapons and the clown handling himself like a movie martial artist. By the time they were broken up, there was so much grease paint and blood on Charlotte's knuckles it looked as though she were wearing gloves made out of horror.

The shrinks would call it a "Stress-Induced Psychotic Episode." Her parents would tell her it happened to everyone with greatness in them. All the excuses and window-dressing wouldn't matter to Clint, though. He was stuck with an unshakable image, that of the only warm person in his life viciously attacking a human whose job was to create laughter. That was what ambition, what desire, did to people; that was what it turned them into. And just like that, Clint was on the path he would walk all the way into adulthood.

*   *   *

Clint stirred, slowly opening his eyes to see the slow wobble of a ceiling fan making its lazy rotation. He was in his bed at the resort, rays of sunset streaming through his window as the last of the storm clouds dispersed from the sky. For the barest of instants, Clint allowed himself to hope it had been a dream. Those hopes were dashed almost before they had fully formed.

Took you long enough. I swear, as little time as you mortals get, you wouldn't think you'd squander so much of it sleeping.

"Who…" Clint stopped himself. There was no need for senseless questions. He'd participated in a ceremony to free a god. The new tenant in his brain was identifiable through a pretty simple process of elimination. "Kodiwandae?"

In the… well, I suppose flesh isn't really the right word, is it? But yes, it is I, the great and powerful Kodiwandae.

"Okay." Clint took a deep breath and found his calm center. In this case it was fortunate that the calm center was the majority of what composed Clint Tucker. "Why are you in my head? Aren't you supposed to be free?"

Freedom is a relative thing. I'm not stuck in a tree anymore, so in a sense, yes, I am free to wander about. However, I haven't regained my power yet, and we gods are shaped by our power, so until the ceremony is finished, I'm afraid I'm still amorphous.

"Complete the ceremony?"

Well, yes; you haven't forgotten already, have you? I know it was in the story you heard. Freeing me is only the first part. You also have to journey to the temple on Denilale and restore my rightful power to me.

"Right… we have to call down the goddess who imprisoned you."

Correct! On that note, we really should get a move on.

"Wait, how did you know I heard about that part of the story?"

Well, you were asleep for a long time. I didn't have anything else to entertain me, so I rifled through your memories a bit, just to get myself up to speed.

"You can read my mind? Makes me feel silly for talking."

No, that part is still important. Reading an active human mind is like trying to read letters swirling in a tornado. Everything is too fluid and too fast-moving to get more than a sense of it. I can only read your memories; those are neatly stored and organized.

"Too bad, that would have been a real time saver." Clint had no idea what he was saying at this point, only that the inane conversation was easier than accepting this voice in his head was really a god, because accepting it meant that he had to take action if he wanted it gone. That seemed too big right now, too momentous a prospect of something to wrap his wee over-occupied brain around.

On the subject of time saving, it's very important we mobilize soon. Your sudden nap has burned up the rest of the day and there's a pretty important matter to attend to.

"Sorry about that. Not sure what happened." Another person might have said this sarcastically. Clint did not.

Oh, it's to be expected. You're fully mortal, after all: not really built for hosting divine energies. That's part of why there had to be someone from a godly bloodline at the offering; they're better suited vessels.

"Should I be concerned?"

Clint couldn't be sure, but he was relatively certain there was a sense of hesitation before the answer came. *Probably not. This is one of those circumstances where haste might be a boon, though.*

"Uh huh." A new thought entered Clint's head, one he probably would have had earlier if not for the series of sudden surprises he kept encountering. "Hey, wait; if you needed a god to do the ceremony and be your transportation, then why are you in me? And who was there that had divine heritage?"

Before an answer could come, the door to Clint's room opened and Thunder walked in, carrying a bottle of water and a handful of what appeared to be aspirin.

"Hey dude, heard you chattering solo in here and figged you were awake. Let's get you medded and bedded before you do any permanent damage. Talking to yourself after eating voltage is a big neg sign."

Clint opened his mouth to explain that he was merely getting his thoughts in order and he appreciated the concern, but when his tongue began to waggle it wasn't his own even voice that burst forth from his throat.

"Oh, I assure you, he isn't crazy. We were merely discussing the logistics of finishing the ceremony and returning me to power."

Thunder dropped the bottle and the aspirin, the pills rolling along the floor in a mad break for freedom. Their triumph would last days, until the rooms were free and the maid-staff swept them into their dustpans and set them off on a new adventure.

"Whoa, bro. Whoa."

"Yeah," Clint said, seizing control of his mouth. "Maybe you'd better get the others. I have a feeling this day isn't over yet."

"Totes."

*　　　*　　　*

Dr. Kaia Hale sat at the hotel bar, downing another glass of whiskey. Kenowains cut their teeth on softer, sweeter alcohols as they grew up, but Kaia had developed an appreciation for the darker drinks as she assimilated to academia. She was a bright girl, and she'd learned very quickly that women who could discuss the nuances of scotch with their male peers advanced more rapidly than those who abstained. Not that this was a whiskey anyone would find worth discussing. It was the house dreck, and Kaia was pouring it down her throat like it was the secret to immortality.

Kaia chuckled to herself. How many of those supposed secrets had she read in her studies? Who knew... well, probably Sober Kaia knew. She wasn't here at the moment, though. Sober Kaia couldn't handle this particular moment in her life, so Drunk Kaia had tagged in to drop a flying elbow on it and send it sprawling to the mat. It wasn't that this moment was really all that bad, either. Sure, a freak electrical storm had cropped up at an inopportune time and shocked that Clint guy, and yes, she'd been so scared she'd hallucinated seeing the electricity come from the tree, but the doc had come and gone and said Clint would be fine. Except for some broken cameras, which the Goodwins would not shut the fuck up about, it was all going to be okay. Hell, even the shoot

86

wasn't lost, thanks to Thunder's lower-quality camera. Score one for analog in the digital world, baby! Kaia would still get paid. Everyone would go home safe and happy. Except…

Kaia drained her glass and motioned for another. Except Kaia wasn't some fucking nervous nelly who got all hysterical at the first sign of lightning. Except Kaia hadn't imagined the way that storm blew up when the ceremony began, no matter what the other islanders told her. Except Kaia knew what she saw, and that golden leaping lightning had come from the tree. The tree where the god was sealed. Where he had been sealed.

Kaia groaned and placed her head on the bar. That was the real crux of the problem, the driving force that had sent Sober Kaia silently screaming down to the bottom of a bottle of truly shitty alcohol. Dr. Kaia Hale had sensed she was committing the cardinal sin of anyone who studied myths and legends. Kaia was stepping onto forbidden ground, going the way of pariahs and madmen, shattering the unspoken taboo. She was wrapping a thread around her finger that would unravel her entire world with a single tug.

Kaia Hale, in deepest chambers of her heart, was beginning to Believe.

*   *   *

"Look, it's not me, I'm telling you," Clint reiterated, stony stares meeting his pleas. The women had proven harder to convince than Thunder, April objecting due to her lack of faith in such nonsense and Falcon holding that since Clint wasn't of divine heritage, he couldn't really be playing cabbie for a god.

"Look, we get that the storm might have messed you up; honestly, we were all amazed when the doctor said the lighting strike hadn't even done any burn damage. But this is bordering on delusional," April said.

"I swear, I've converted mountains that were more pliable than you two."

"See, right there is the first hole in your story: if that voice is supposed to be an ancient god trapped for centuries, then why does he speak English?"

Clint paused; he hadn't stopped to think about that. The first time he'd heard Kodiwandae speak he'd understood the meaning but not the words. Since he woke up, the voice in his head had been speaking perfect English, even using phrases Clint was familiar with.

"The boy here was out for a good few hours; I had ample time to familiarize myself with his modern language."

Clint gave the room a shrug as the voice spoke. He supposed if it could rifle through his memories, it made about as much sense for the god to be able to learn his native tongue.

"Clint, I know you had quite an experience, but you should really cease with this blasphemy," Falcon cautioned. "Only one with the right lineage would be judged worthy. You don't think you're a god, do you?"

"Of course I'm not-"

"*Of course he's not a god! Watch your mouth before accusing others of blasphemy, little miss. There was a god present, though, so the ceremony counted.*"

"Then why are you in Clint?"

"*I sort of... kind of... missed.*"

"Gods don't miss."

"*Look, I don't know where you get your theology, but if my kind were infallible I wouldn't bloody well be in this mess to begin with, now would I?*" Clint felt a strange balloon of stress welling in his head, a foreign experience to him that was profoundly uncomfortable. He began to suspect Kodiwandae was getting defensive.

"Calm down, Clint," April cautioned.

"I'm totally calm."

"*Well, I'm not; I'm cranky after spending the last few centuries in that tree and now the first thing I have to deal with once I'm out is doubters. I don't have time for this. You there, old one."* Clint felt a strange sensation, like a hand was rummaging around in the lower part of his brain. *"Falcon, right? Come here and put your hand on Clint's."*

"What are you doing?" Clint asked.

Saving us three hours of philosophical discussion. These words were only spoken in Clint's head.

"But you can't read minds."

Current events are never as useful as history. Trust me on that one.

Falcon raised an eyebrow, which Clint met with a confused expression of his own. She debated, but ultimately decided no matter how delusional the young man was acting, he still didn't seem dangerous. Maybe if she played along with his fantasy she could help bring him out of it.

Falcon crossed the few feet between them and placed her hand into Clint's outstretched fingers. There was a light shock, like he had rubbed stocking feet along the carpet before their skin made contact, then a strange sense in her head. It was impossible to accurately describe; the closest Falcon could come would be to say it was like the feeling you got that someone was watching you, only from the inside.

"There we are. Your real name is Valerie Quinn, you've been married twice and both husbands are deceased. You love steak with a fiery passion, which has made being vegan a special brand of hell. You lost your virginity on March fourth-"

Falcon leapt away as though Clint had kicked her in the shin. She stared at him, his dull brown eyes looking apologetic while his mouth twisted up into a wry smirk.

"Godly enough for you?"

Falcon nodded; her tongue had momentarily gone dumb. With enough time and research Clint could have procured most, but not all, of that information. He hadn't had that time, though; he'd been asleep since the strike, and even if he'd been faking, there was no Internet in any of the rooms.

"Okay, that was kind of weird, I'll give you," April said cautiously. "But that doesn't mean I'm ready to jump on the 'Clint is carting around Kodiwandae' bandwagon."

"Might as well give it a swirly. God-carting is the best we've got," Thunder pointed out.

"No, it's a random myth that happens to fit a variety of circumstances. It doesn't mesh with reality, though, so it's a bunk idea off the bat."

"Isn't the basis of sound science looking at all the data and allowing it to direct one to a functional conclusion? What you're doing is trying to force this new information to fit into an unproven hypothesis you've already formulated," Thunder pointed out.

If Clint's memory reading trick had stunned the room, Thunder's outburst left it absolutely flabbergasted. After considerable time, April broke the shocked silence.

"Where did you hear that?"

"My bros at the frat house and I used to power hour to documentaries over stuff in our classes so we could get our drink on while still logging study hours. I remember that from a really long one about the origins of the scientific method. I pulled a puker on the couch by the credits."

"O-kay. Well, you've got a point, I think. I don't know what's going on, and I guess it would be closed-minded of me to assume anything at this point."

"Great, glad we're all on the same page. Now then, if someone can grab the pear, we should all really be on our way."

"The pear?" April asked.

"Yes, the pear. The one you used in the ceremony. The one that contained the last vestiges of my power so I can call Nature in her temple. You did grab the pear, didn't you?"

There was a series of awkward glances and some uncomfortable shuffling.

"The rain was balls out crazytown after you got shocked," Thunder said softly.

"It seemed imperative to get back to the bus," April added.

"Perfect. Just perfect. What else can go wrong?"

10.

Lawrence did not dream, neither in his sleep nor in his waking hours. Schemed, plotted, planned: all of those were frequent occurrences, but dreaming was the stuff of fantasy, and Lawrence had no need for that unless he was crafting one for someone else. So it was with some surprise he found himself in a lush jungle near the beach when he distinctly remembered settling in for a light nap some time earlier.

"Curious," Lawrence said. He checked his shoes and his attire, confirming it was his usual suit and wingtips. Since he was not already dripping in sweat from the tropical heat despite being swathed in wool, it seemed an obvious conclusion that this event was not occurring in reality.

"Kneel mortal, for you are in the presence of the mighty god Felbren." The voice seemed to echo out from the trees all around; pinning down an actual initialization point was clearly impossible. Lawrence gave a half-hearted glance around, but it was mostly for show. Anyone who went to that much trouble to conceal their audible location wasn't going to be standing in plain sight.

"Thank you, but I think that would muddy my slacks. I'd prefer to stand."

"You… impudent mortal! Do you not understand what has befallen you?"

"Quite well, actually. Either I'm dreaming, in which case there is no real concern, or you are truly the god Felbren, in which case I have nothing to fear."

"Nothing to fear? You are a fool, little mortal. The great god Felbren has visited his will upon your kind since before your bloodline had even begun."

"No question. But the fact remains that I'm on Kenowai and Felbren is bound to Faldilonda; therefore I am beyond his reach."

"What, um, what makes you say that?"

Lawrence smiled, making no particular effort to have the expression appear more jovial than it was. He'd only been taking a guess, but he'd hit his mark. "I listened to the story and paid attention."

"It was only a story."

"All tales of the mythical beings we call gods are only stories. If I'm extending you the cordiality of believing you exist, then I must make similar assumptions about the legends regarding you."

The trees in front of Lawrence parted and a glowing man with a round face and an ornate white and green outfit stepped forward. He eyed Lawrence warily then waved his hand. Where once there had only been dirt and vegetation now stood two cushy chairs with a table between them. On the table was a bottle of red wine and a pair of goblets, ornate and ancient by the look of them.

"Humans like you take all the fun out of this." Felbren motioned for Lawrence to sit, and this time he complied.

"My apologies. I've never been visited by a higher being before."

"No wonder. You're as empty a vessel as a bone cup in the desert. I've seen rocks with more Belief than you."

"It would be difficult for me to disagree with you. That does beg the question, though; why am I being graced with such an honor as your visit?"

Felbren grabbed the wine bottle and removed the cork with two fingers. It was the kind of thing physics would never allow in the rational world, but physics hadn't been invited to this party. *"Cut the flattery bullshit. I've got worshippers for that."* Felbren filled his own goblet to the brim then poured a glass for Lawrence.

"Fine. What do you want?"

"Ah, now that's why I'm visiting you, right to the quick of things. You might not have any Belief, but you can

assimilate new information and utilize it to your advantage like none other."

"How do you know that?"

"My kind always keeps tabs on people like you - fixers, as you call yourselves. There is a place in our ranks for the devout, the earnest, the loving, even the moronic. People with your kind of ruthlessness and intellect, though, well, it's proven beneficial to know what you were up to even if you don't fit into our hierarchy."

Lawrence tried the wine. There weren't enough ideas in all the languages of the world to describe it, let alone enough words. If Lawrence were the kind of man who could be moved, he would have wept in overwhelming joy. Instead he set the glass down and met the god's eyes.

"So we come back to it: what do you need?" Lawrence had gathered that whatever had gotten Felbren to play ball this long was far more than a mere want.

"Your people freed Kodiwandae. This is inconvenient for me since I haven't completed everything I wanted to get done in his absence."

"You mean convincing the woman he loves to love you instead."

"Anyway, I'm here because while he is free, he isn't yet restored. This creates a narrow window of opportunity to slow his full recovery, buying me the time I need."

"How do you stop a god from rising?"

"Take away its yeast. Sorry, old joke among the pantheon. Somewhat apt analogy, though. Kodiwandae cannot rise again until he calls Nature to restore his realm. For that he needs the last of the energy he had when he was sealed."

"And how do I get that?"

"Oh no, cunning one, not so easy. I won't be telling you that little tidbit until we have a bargain."

Lawrence smiled again and took another sip of his wine. Felbren had seen looks like that many a time, almost always attached to one of Iohalo's deep beasties, the kind that lived far down in the dark waters and all but the most unfortunate humans had yet to uncover.

"Then let us deal."

*　　　*　　　*

Finding a ride to the pear was proving tougher than expected. It seemed that the locals weren't particularly keen on making the drive to Kodiwandae's tree, especially not with foreigners, and extra especially not at night. The front desk clerk told them in kind but unyielding tones that the resort would not risk the lives and vehicles of their shuttle service by sending them up that road in the dark. It probably didn't help that Clint kept mumbling to himself, trying to convince Kodiwandae that yelling at his servants to do as they were told would cause more problems than it would solve. Of course, all everyone else saw was a white kid with his head down and a constant stream of words mumbling forth. It was off-putting, to say the least.

They might have spent all night cajoling and pleading with locals if not for a bit of mercy from the King of Kenowai.

"Ow!" Clint yelped. He whirled around to see the cat that had been with them on the bus casually walking out the door as though he hadn't just sunk his teeth into Clint's ankle.

Follow the cat.

"Why?"

"Why what?" April asked.

Because I say so. He wanted your attention, now follow him.

"That's crazy."

"Oh, he's talking to Kodiwandae." April paused and realized that she had just taken a person having a conversation with someone in their head as an explanation

99

rather than a curiosity. Maybe Clint was right without meaning to be; maybe this was crazy.

If you have any better ideas I'm open to hearing them.

"I do, actually; we go back upstairs and go to sleep and I forget this whole thing ever happened."

"Dude, your decibels are starting to creep vertically," Thunder cautioned him.

Rousing idea. Then some passer-by takes the pear and I'm stuck inside you until your fleshy form falls apart.

Clint took a deep breath. "We're going after the cat."

Wish I'd thought of that.

"Shut up."

Clint walked quickly, both to close the gap that had occurred in the time spent debating and to get clear of the hotel before any of the other guests started getting too concerned about his seemingly solo conversations. He might not have cared what people thought of him, but he wasn't so dense that he didn't know enough people thinking you were crazy meant a one-way ticket to a padded room all of your own.

The other three tagged along gamely. At this point it would be hard to say if the sum of their loyalty came from fear, curiosity, or guilt, but they came all the same and Clint was glad for it. He'd never been particularly big on needing people; however, it turned out that in big enough situations, even he enjoyed the comfort of people having his back.

To the left.

The voice snapped Clint from his reverie and back to the task at hand. The cat was weaving through grass, invisible in the night sky with the exception of its golden tail tip. It padded out past the swimming pool, through the grass around the tennis courts, and out to the edge of the hotel's property. Here there were smaller buildings, squat apartment complexes with some stone benches and a few fire pits for grilling. It was clearly where the help lived, though most were still on shift, leaving the place looking abandoned. The cat didn't head toward the housing section of the buildings; instead it kept walking toward a wooden garage with a corrugated metal roof.

"Is anyone else wondering how that cat made it back here already?" April wondered as they skulked along.

"He ran away several hours ago," Falcon pointed out.

"Yeah, but that clearing is a good twenty miles from here. Who ever heard of a cat covering that sort of distance in half a day?"

"We're trailing said cat at the insistence of the god currently trapped in our friend's head so that we might find the enchanted pear that will set him free. Perhaps it is time to accept that there are many mysteries and bits of magic this island holds."

"Touché."

"Shh," Clint whispered. The cat had gone inside the garage, and now that they were closer they could see a faint light shining through the poorly-aligned slats of wood making up the walls. They heard a voice shortly after the golden tail tip was lost from sight.

"My King, two nights in a row you visit. You do me too much honor."

"Oh coolness, it's Mano," Thunder said, walking forward eagerly and going into the garage. The others hurriedly went after him, both because it was clearly where they were meant to go and because no one quite trusted Thunder to represent them to the locals.

As soon as Clint stepped into the garage he saw it: a rusted, beat up, barely recognizable old pickup truck. It looked like Father Time had caught this vehicle messing around with his daughter and come after it with appropriate vengeance. Clint was almost eighty percent sure that even standing in the same room as this thing should require a tetanus shot.

Mano was sitting on a work bench next to it. The cat stared up at the newcomers with an innocent tilt of the head, as though it hadn't just herded them here like cattle.

"Oh, hello, folks," Mano said, standing up quickly. "Did you get turned around? You're of course welcome to be here, but I'm afraid there isn't much to do, especially compared to the main grounds."

Clint opened his mouth to thank Mano for the hospitality and apologize for the intrusion while assuring him that they would be on their way now. Predictably, this is not what happened.

"Hey kid, does that thing run?"

*   *   *

"This had better be about compensation for our equipment," Dustin warned from the doorway. His brother, who was lounging on the couch, straightened up as Lawrence stepped in. Lawrence was dressed in his usual attire with two exceptions: he'd left the tie off the ensemble and he carried a battered old video camera under his arm. Not that Lawrence was one to dismiss curious event as mere anomalous dream, but he was not the type of man to undertake things without some sense of confirmation. Luckily, Thunder, for all his faults, could point a camera where the action was happening and hold it there when hell broke loose. Viewing the only remaining footage had confirmed that something strange had definitely taken place, and it meshed enough with Felbren's description for Lawrence to lend credence to the god's claims.

"As a matter of fact, it is." Lawrence walked over to a free chair and took a seat. Some businessmen he'd dealt with liked to stay standing when dealing with peons, to remind them who the more powerful person in the room was. Lawrence was of the opinion that if you needed tricks to convince others you were more powerful then you probably weren't. "It seems you boys, while excellent photographers, are shit at negotiations."

"Beg pardon?" Justin sat forward on the couch.

"Oh, you managed to get your pay rate to an impressive level, I'll give you that; but the cost was several smaller benefits. For example: any assumption of risk to your equipment on behalf of the company."

"You're lying," Dustin accused.

"Go read the contract; or better yet, have a lawyer read it to you. He'll tell you that not only are we not liable for a dime on replacing your cameras, we also don't have to pay you for the shoot since you failed to deliver any product."

"That's ridiculous! We failed because our gear was destroyed in the storm that you sent us into!" Dustin was growing red in the face while Justin watched calmly.

"Correction: you sent yourself into it. You were hired as independent contractors. That means production of footage, as well as personal safety measures, were all on your head. So far as Camelot Burgers is concerned, all you did was take a plane ticket and a hotel lodging while providing us with nothing in return."

"Why, you son of a bit-"

"Shut up." Justin cut his brother off before Dustin's rage could reach a crescendo. "I assume you have something else to tell us, otherwise you'd have let the lawyers relay this message."

Lawrence adjusted his regard of the quieter Goodwin brother. He'd taken him for shy at the outset, but it seemed he was merely smart enough to know when to stay silent. That made him both more useful and more dangerous.

"I have a new job for you: one that pays high enough to take care of your lost cameras and cover your initial fee. This, like the other, is performance-based. No delivery, no compensation, pure and simple."

"Why should we trust you when you've already screwed us once?" Dustin snapped.

105

"One, I didn't screw you; you screwed yourself through poor observation of fine print. Two, given the cost of such powerful cameras and the relatively low liquidity of your company's assets, I seem to be your best option by far."

Justin leaned forward on his couch and met Lawrence's eyes, a feat few men had managed more than once. "I dislike that you know about our business. I dislike that you have backed us into a corner. I sincerely dislike the attitude with which you've come to us. All of that said, I have to agree that your offer is the best option before us so far. Now, let's hear the details and I'll tell you if we're in."

"Double the agreed-upon fee and reimbursement of full retail cost to replace every piece of equipment damaged in the electrical storm."

Dustin snickered. "Sure, and who do we have to kill for that kind of money?"

"If it were just murder the price would be far lower. No, what you have to do has the potential of being a bit more complex." Lawrence didn't lean forward, didn't shift his position, didn't make any overt alternations to his facial expression. None the less, Justin found his courage suddenly wavering and he looked away from the older man's eyes. Something in those eyes had changed, and it elevated the stare to a level Justin couldn't handle.

"You two have been charged with the important task of bringing me a pear."

"That's it? There are, like, ten in the welcome basket; take your pick," Dustin offered.

Lawrence shook his head. "Let me explain. This is a very special pear."

*   *   *

"Fucksocks!" Thunder yelled from the bed of the pickup as a particularly violent bump sent him and Clint airborne. April and Falcon were squished into the cab of the rust machine with Mano and the cat. Since there wasn't enough room for everyone, it was decided that the women and the driver were the logical choices for the safer seating. Clint was beginning to regret the chivalry as they bounced and bounded along the winding road.

Wheeeee!

Kodiwandae was somewhat less concerned, the exhilaration at such rapid movements overtaking any sense of fear he might have absorbed from Clint. In a strange way it was comforting; the mere idea of a god squealing with joy at a bouncing ride was so bizarre it made the whole experience seem surreal. This worked out, because if there was one time Clint needed a little distance from reality, this would be it.

If the road had been dangerous in a passenger bus and by the light of the sun, then climbing it in a nearly-dead truck at night was as suicidal as an antifreeze-chugging competition. Whether it was by blind luck, Mano's driving skill, or divine intervention, they were making progress inch by terrifying inch.

Convincing Mano had actually been the first easy thing they'd dealt with all day. After hearing Kodiwandae's voice, he'd given a courteous nod, started the engine, and motioned for them to pile in.

On the way, April had been explaining the events leading up to their meeting, to which Mano was dutifully listening and answering with an occasional "Uh huh." If she was expecting resistance, she didn't find any. Mano simply absorbed what he was being told and kept his eyes on the road. It wasn't that he was particularly gullible or stupid; it was simply that Mano was a good judge of character with an open mind. The tight-wound girl clearly wasn't lying, so maybe they really had freed Kodiwandae. Mano had made friends with a shark using half a cheap beer: he wasn't one to start lecturing people about the impossible.

"I think I might be sick," Clint said as they took a tight curve, throwing he and Thunder to the other side of the truck's bed.

"Pukers go starboard, por favor."

I forbid you from such an act while I am here. It seems unpleasant.

"I don't get much say in the matter."

"Dude, you can still take aim."

"No, sorry, Thunder, not you. I'll try to go over the side. I was taking to Kodiwandae."

"Ohhh; you should put a finger on the forehead when you're doing inner chatter. Then we'd be copacetic."

"That's actually a good idea. I'll start doing that when I can use my hands again." The extremities in question were currently coiled around the lip of the bed in a white-knuckled grip to hang on.

"Word." Thunder's hands were a mirror image of Clint's.

The truck kept bounding along, meeting various obstacles and hurtling past them by the sheer gift of knowing it would fall apart soon anyway, and if some silly tree wanted to get in its way then that just meant company on the journey to the object afterlife. There's a power in genuinely not giving a fuck, one that extends to the sentient and inanimate alike.

At last, after several close calls including a low hanging branch that Clint would swear took a few inches off his hair, the truck burst forth into the familiar clearing.

Clint and Thunder dropped onto the moonlit grass and panted, physically and mentally exhausted from the ordeal of living through the drive.

"Thank God we're alive," Clint mumbled.

You're welcome.

"Funny; real funny. Let's get on with this."

Clint pulled himself up and looked over at the tree. The others unloaded from the cab and gazed at it too, the light from the stars twinkling through the branches and falling upon the stone altar and the pool of water in its basin. The rock was still there, too, a dark spot in an otherwise silvery surface. They could see it with perfect clarity, because there was nothing on top of it to obscure their vision. No pear, save for the ones still swaying softly on the limbs.

"Fucksocks," Clint swore.

11.

Sprinkles stared out across his island from atop the hill which had once imprisoned Kodiwandae. The humans were still by the altar, bickering about what to do next. They would scramble back and forth from idea to idea like rats climbing a rolling cheese wheel. Sprinkles had never understood the decision making process of non-feline creatures. For him, it was simple: you laid out the facts and reached the appropriate conclusion. That's what he was doing as he watched the trees waving in the wind, greeting their hilltop king as he watched over them.

Sprinkles had to accept that the dilemma these humans currently faced was his fault. Had he not been present, Kodiwandae would not be romping about in one of their minds. Sprinkles hadn't known that at the time, but it didn't excuse him. They would likely blunder about without his assistance; look at how inept they'd proven at even getting here. Recovering the pear was going to be much harder; Sprinkles could already sense that it was no longer on his island. He could feel the direction it had wandered off in, though; once he'd gotten to the site he'd picked up the trail. The pear was already some distance away, past the edge of his kingdom. Sprinkles was under no delusions. This chase would likely take him away from the island. He liked the island: it was warm and pleasant and the people showed him the proper respect.

Still, Sprinkles was not only a cat and a godling, nor was he merely some icon for the people to bow to. Sprinkles was a King, and as King, he felt the weight of responsibility for his people and his actions. He'd caused this to happen to guests on his island. He would do whatever it required to set things right. That was the burden of the crown.

The dark cat rose from his sitting position and took one last glance at the land below. He had not left his island for a very long time. Perhaps it would be a good thing. Cats are ill-equipped to shrug, but Sprinkles was not only a cat, so shrug he did. His choice was made; all that remained was to see what came of it. He turned and began heading back to the five humans and the one impotent god.

*   *   *

"Maybe we can draw it out and trap it in a gourd," April ventured.

"No one is putting me in a damned gourd! If I'm going to be stuck, I'll take a prison cell that can at least drink away its troubles."

"Plus, I'm pretty sure that's a different mythology," Falcon pointed out.

"Perhaps we can appeal to another of the gods to help," Mano suggested.

"Are you kidding? Look, this is embarrassing enough. For my kind, being powerless is the equivalent of you shitting your pants at a wedding. It's the sort of shame you never live down."

"All of the islanders know the story of Kodiwandae," Mano said.

"Yes, but that's just humans. I can always show up and deny it, say I went on a good bender with some mountain gods for a few centuries."

"No way that'll fly, bro; they'll know you're all up in liar town." Thunder was lounging on the grass, looking at the stars, the least wound up of all of them at the moment.

"Well, of course they'll know. They won't be able to prove it, though, so it doesn't matter."

"So what, you're just going to knock around in my brain until I die and then float around freely?" Clint asked.

"Might as well."

"That's insane; how is being trapped better than asking some other god for help?"

"You don't really grasp the timeline of immortals. We have the advantage of being able to wait out most problems. Sooner or later, there will be a solution."

"Maybe for you, but Clint spends the rest of his life with a mental hitchhiker," April said.

"Look, you're the ones who did the ceremony and forgot to pick up the pear. This is hardly my fault."

"No one told us about grabbing the pear," Falcon said. "Kaia left out any mention of needing it after the ceremony was done."

"Then be mad at this Kaia woman."

"I think there's enough blame to go around," Clint mumbled,

Sprinkles did not mew to announce his presence as he re-joined the group. Such things were unnecessary. His presence announced itself more effectively than any minor yelp could ever dare hope to. He slipped between them, the towering legs supporting unsure minds, gliding like the fog over to Clint's side. Sprinkles took a seat and waited. He didn't have to wait for long.

"The cat knows where the pear is heading."

"The cat? How the hell does the cat know?" April asked.

"Well, he is the King of Kenowai," Mano said.

"Oh yeah, one of the bartenderinos mentioned there was a royal kitty running around," Thunder recalled.

"Your people have a fascinating system of rulership," Falcon observed, trying as best she could to phrase it complimentarily.

"Actually, we have a governor we elect every three years. The whole 'King of Kenowai' thing is just a running joke among the islanders."

"*No, it isn't.*"

"I've lived here all my life. I'm positive that cat is the one we call the King."

"*It is. I just meant it wasn't a joke.*"

"So the cat is actually the ruler of the island?" Even Falcon sounded a bit dubious now.

"*In that it manages daily bureaucracy? No. But it does keep the island running smoothly, and right now it wants to help us.*"

"I thought you said minds were too messy to read," Clint accused. "Plus, I have to be touching someone for you to peek in their brain."

"*Human minds are; animals are another story. Besides, the cat is special.*"

115

"It is?" Clint sounded dubious.

"I haven't met too many animals that were royalty," Falcon pointed out.

"*That, too.*"

Clint contemplated objecting, then realized he'd come this far into the land of insanity - he may as well stamp his passport and accept his citizenship. "Okay, so the cat can lead us to the pear. How do we get him to start?"

On cue, Sprinkles rose from the ground and ambled over to the beat up truck, nearly forgotten in the rush of panic. He climbed through the open door and across the threadbare seat, leaping up onto the dashboard and settling in. With minimal movement, the golden tip of his tail swung forward, pointing toward the east end of the island, the opposite side from where they had come from.

"Kitters is a pointer," Thunder surmised, leaping into the bed of the truck without even a hint of fear despite the experience he'd endured less than an hour ago.

"This feels too easy," Clint said.

Think of it this way: finding the pear is only half the battle. We still have to get it away from whoever knew enough to take it.

Clint stuck his index and middle finger to his forehead. "I guess that's a fair point."

"Who are you saluting?" April asked.

"No one; this is my way of saying I'm talking to Kodiwandae so you guys don't get confused. It was Thunder's idea."

"It's like the siggie you use when you're getting chatty out of character mid-game," Thunder called from the truck.

"Wait, what?" Clint stared at the man in the pink polo, uncertain he'd heard correctly.

"Nothin', bro, don't worry about it. Let's vamoose!"

"We're so sorry to impose on your generosity, but would you mind taking us a bit farther?" Falcon said, her old hippie eyes opened extra wide as she asked Mano. The tan man gave her a smile.

"You have the god and the King of my island with you. It is an honor to drive you wherever you need to go."

Mano meant it, too, or at least he did if any of this was true. If it wasn't, then these people were bat-shit crazy and the last thing he wanted to do was piss them off. Alone. In the woods. In the middle of the night. Without having told anyone where he was going. Had Kodiwandae been in full possession of his abilities, he would have felt Mano drop a prayer in his direction as the true weight of the situation fell upon those muscular shoulders. There was nothing to do but press on, though, so Mano pulled the keys from his pocket and sat behind the wheel.

"I'm sure we'll find the pear and help you regain your glory," Falcon said before getting into the cab.

"Plus, we'll get rid of your little squatter," April tossed in, giving Clint a warm smile. It might very well have been the first non-measured thing he'd seen her do since their meeting. He didn't know if that made it more encouraging or depressing.

Squatter? You mortals have really let your understanding of respect slip since I've been gone.

"I'm sure she meant it in the nicest possible way."

Oh, well, in that case I suppose I can let it slide.

Clint couldn't really tell if Kodiwandae didn't get sarcasm or was just screwing with him, so he let the question fall out of his mind. He walked over and climbed into the bed, bracing himself for another jarring journey. He wondered what happened if you died in a car crash while shuttling a god around. Maybe there was some special consideration for that scenario in the afterlife.

Clint almost smacked himself on the forehead. The afterlife! And why they were here, and why bad things happened to good people, and every other impossible question he'd ever faced. He'd been so stuck on the downside of his situation that Clint hadn't stopped long enough to realize that he was plugged in to someone who could give him answers to the unanswerable questions mankind faced.

His face twisted into a very un-Clint-like smirk. So Kodiwandae wanted their help in returning him to power. He wanted to ride around in Clint's head. He wanted them to go on some insane goose chase for a pear. Fine, fine to all of it. But Kodiwandae was about to start paying some rent.

*   *   *

The boat captain was uncomfortable with his new passengers. It could be the way they seemed to communicate without words, or how their eyes said quite plainly that everything they saw was beneath them. It especially might have been the way they'd simply walked up to him, held out a stack of bills, and told him where to go. In his experience, these sorts of enterprises almost always involved drug deals or body disposal, though he was fine with either so long as the body in question wasn't his. These were the odd jobs one had to take in a tourist-driven economy. Sometimes people wanted to go watch dolphins swim among the waves, other times they just wanted to exchange cocaine for cash. The customer was always right.

"I still think we should have searched around for her more," Dustin whispered to his brother, their conversation concealed by the splashing sounds of the boat pushing through the water.

"You heard the charter captain: a woman matching her description booked passage on the last ship of the day to Alendola."

"The description was just of a tall, pretty island woman who seemed completely wasted. Besides, why would she take the pear to a neighboring island instead of where the temple is?"

"I don't know, Dustin. If I did, I'd have a better idea of how to intercept her. She essentially has a doctorate in mythology, though; we have to face the possibility that she knows some use for the sealed power that we don't. She was smart enough to grab it, after all."

Thunder's camera had captured more than just Clint's apparent electrocution. As the spiky-haired youth had rushed forward to help his lighting-injured friend, his video camera had continued rolling. It had captured video evidence of their immediate panic and calling for the driver, it had documented them loading the unconscious body into the bus, and in a few key frames, it had recorded a thin, tan woman removing a pear that seemed to be emitting a soft glow from the altar and then stuffing it into her backpack.

The brothers Goodwin already knew what the others had wasted precious time in learning: the pear of Kodiwandae was no longer at his tree. Rather than burn time trying to backtrack to the starting point, Dustin and Justin had inquired after Kaia in the hotel bar, learning she had been tying off a powerful drunk for some hours before eventually being cut off and stumbling out into the night. It had taken some time on the phone and a few quick lies to the island's only cab company, but they eventually learned she had been taken to the nearest port. They also learned she had talked the cabbie's ear off about theology and puked her meager lunch onto the back seat. The office clerk was still yelling about getting someone to pay for the cleaning when they hung up the phone and headed for the docks.

Now they sat on a small fishing boat with a captain who kept glancing back at them and muttering something about "just keep it hidden" before checking his instruments and making necessary corrections.

"If she's got some master plan then why is she apparently so drunk?" Dustin wondered aloud.

"Obviously she's faking to keep anyone from getting suspicious. If you were trying to sneak away with something like that, what's a better cover than acting like a blundering alcoholic grappling with an existential crisis? It's quite brilliant; if we hadn't watched her take the pear we would have never suspected her."

"Cunning bitch."

"Quite. Still, no need to worry. The locals said the kiddies are looking back at the altar and there is no way the girl knows we're on to her. If we move quickly, we can recover the pear before anyone even knows we're in the game."

The boat captain was beginning to lean his suspicions toward drug deal, though why they kept using such a ridiculous code word as "pear" was beyond him. Then again, he was getting on in years and couldn't keep track with all the phrases today's youth used. Just last year he'd tried to score some of this "Twitter" everyone kept mentioning. The dealer, his nephew, had stared at him for some time before reaching into his bag and pulling out a small bag of green, leafy product. It hadn't been bad, but the captain hadn't seen what all the fuss was about.

"How much longer to Alendola?" One of them, the chattier one, was antsy.

"Two hours with a good wind."

"And what about if we get a rough wind?"

The captain smiled at him, his normally easygoing nature stretched especially thin by the night's bullshit. "This is a small boat on big seas. We get too rough a wind and your arrival time depends on how well you can swim."

"Sit down," the other brother commanded the fidgety one. "We're in no hurry. She'll have let her guard down by the time her vessel lands. We can afford to be calm and precise."

The captain shook his head as he adjusted his bearings. One day he was going to get out of this business and take up a career with fewer skullduggeries and under-the-table dealings. Maybe he'd try politics.

*　　　*　　　*

How should I know?

"What do you mean, 'how should you know'? You're a god; isn't this the kind of stuff you folks are generally keyed in on?"

Clint wasn't bothering with the forehead touching as the rusty truck bounced along the unpaved roads. Thunder had momentarily dozed off, lulled by the unsecured truck bed's gentle rocking, and there was no way the others could hear him in the cab over the guttural screech of the engine doing its damnedest to hold together.

Well, some stuff, sure, but how would I know where you all came from?

"Didn't gods create us?"

Probably not. Not my kind of gods anyway.

"There are different types?"

Yes and no. My kind is comprised of gods who are formed and shaped by the Beliefs that you people have. Humans might be weak, surly little creatures, but that capacity of yours to put stock in something unseen and unproven is a magic like nothing else I've ever seen.

"So, wait, you exist because people think you exist?"

That is an incredibly simplified way of putting it, but yes. Mortal's Belief is what manifests us initially. Their Wants direct and power us, showing us the greatest desires they have. Spending our time and power to grant some of them leads them to have even stronger Belief. It's a mutually beneficial relationship.

"Okay, so what about the other type?"

Those are the ones who might be shaped by Belief, but they'll exist whether humans are here or not. Nature, Time, Life, Death, even Fate. Those are things that keep the entire world in running order. Probably more worlds than just ours, though that's merely conjecture. Hang on; let me find a good analogy. Clint felt that strange digging sensation in the back of his head again. He was beginning to get used to it, and that worried him more than the feeling itself. *Here we go. Think of it as humans are office grunts and my kind is middle management. We've got more freedom than you do, and you're generally subject to our whims, but if you all quit we'd be up shit creek.*

124

"I see. So the others are upper management?"

No, the others are the building.

"How does that work?"

Look, if all the grunts quit, middle management would be fucked; this would in turn leave upper management screwed and so on and so on because they all exist in a relationship that depends on one another. The building doesn't need any of them, though. The building will be there whether it's full or empty: it is constant.

"If it's empty long enough, someone could tear it down."

Follow that train of thought, let me know how those sleepless nights work out for you.

"Okay, fine; so whoever made the world would have predated you, since you didn't exist until humans thought you up."

Bingo.

"What about these bigger beings? The constant ones. Didn't you ever get curious and ask one of them?"

The last time I met one of those beings she ripped me from my power and stuck me in a tree.

"I thought that was a local goddess?"

No, they have a local name for her, but it was Nature. Every earth goddess is Nature; they just use different terms for her.

"Sort of like how every culture has its own version of the Grim Reaper?"

You catch on quick. Yeah, those are all Death.

"Seems like it would get confusing."

Only because names matter to you. They don't give a damn what you call them anymore than they care if you believe in them.

"Because they are Constant." Clint was finally wrapping his head around this unexpected divine hierarchy.

The lucky fucks. Clint didn't hear the bitterness in Kodiwandae's voice as much as he felt it, rippling through him as though it had come from his own frustrations. The emotions Kodiwandae felt were unsettling to Clint, much more tumultuous and quick-changing than his usual monochrome pallet. Clint had endeavored all his life to avoid these spurts of anger and annoyance, yet here they were, raising his blood pressure all the same.

"What about the bigger gods? The ones whose religions have billions of followers?"

Most of them are nice enough, though a bit full of themselves. In all fairness, when you've got that many people kissing your ass it's sort of hard not to develop an ego.

"I meant-"

I know what you meant. Gods, even big gods, come and go. There have been others before and there will likely be different ones in the future.

"Okay, different subject; what about the afterlife?"

Can't tell you.

"You don't know about that either?"

No, that one I know all about. I can tell you what the rules of my religion state, but I can't give you any inside information on it.

"Why not?"

Just one of the rules for gods. Part of living is the uncertainty of not knowing what comes next. The Constant in charge laid down that law long before I came around.

"I thought gods were above the rules."

Then you haven't been listening. Nature did this to me for picking a flower she said not to. What do you think Death would do if I broke his cardinal commandment by spilling the beans?

"Oh."

'Oh' is right.

"Geez, is there anything you can tell me I don't already know?"

There are five individual species of squirrel living on Kenowai.

"Not exactly what I meant."

Then maybe you should start being more specific.

Clint turned his head and looked at the shoreline they were steadily drawing closer to. He'd been all jazzed up at the idea of getting to peek behind the metaphysical curtain, and now he was finding out the universe worked on as much bureaucracy as the companies he got fired from. The most depressing part of that revelation was when Clint realized the he wasn't even all that surprised.

The truck began to slow as the sounds of waves crashing against the shore reached Clint's ears. Mano killed the struggling engine and suddenly it was like a bucket of peace had been poured on the world. Gone was the sputtering and shaking; all that remained in its place was the music of the sea and the wind.

The cat leapt from the cab and padded across the sandy grass, coming to the peak of a dune and pointing his tail across the waters. It was a comical, enjoyable moment, or it would have been if the message weren't clear: the pear was no longer on the island.

The others disembarked from the truck, even Thunder rousing at the voluminous silence. They gathered together by the cat and stared at the dark, choppy waters rocking the small white boats tethered in the harbor. It was Falcon who said what they were all thinking as they watched the moon's reflection in the waves.

"So, now what?"

12.

Lawrence was enjoying a breakfast of poached eggs, crisp ham, and fresh fruit. He was even branching out from his usual practice of drinking only water and washing it all down with a cold glass of orange juice. It was a good day: things were rolling along nicely, and he had enough spare time to properly nourish himself before the many tasks ahead. One of the waiters at the resort restaurant slid up to the side of Lawrence's table and refilled his juice. That accomplished, the dark-haired service professional laid a plain white envelope down by the salt and pepper.

"Your passage has been booked for this afternoon at one, sir. Are you sure you don't want to catch the earlier boat at nine? I inquired with the charter captain and there was still plenty of room."

Lawrence courteously finished chewing before tendering his response. "Thank you, but I'm sure. There are some things I'd like to see on Kenowai before I begin exploring other locales."

"Of course, sir. Can I get you anything else?"

"More cantaloupe, when you have the time."

"Right away."

Lawrence enjoyed the meat and eggs more than the fruit, but his cardiologist had been quite specific on tempering his appetite with more wholesome fare so as not to put his heart in danger. Lawrence enjoyed life, both the current quality and expected quantity, and saw no reason to ignore the warning and decrease either. Of course, if things with Felbren came together as planned, there would be no need for such concerns; however, years of experience had taught Lawrence the benefits of pessimism. Work to succeed, plan for setbacks. Never failures; only setbacks.

Lawrence speared another piece of salty pig flesh and crunched on it cheerfully. Yes indeed, this had the potential to be a good day.

*   *   *

"I'm the king of world!"

"Shhh, be quiet, Thunder; Clint finally fell asleep," April chastised.

"My bad."

"Whatever."

April was beginning to feel the stress of the last day and her nerves were fraying as a result. The five humans

131

and one cat were bobbing along in a medium-sized boat - Thunder had traded a Rolex with a local fisherman who'd shown up a few hours before daylight to begin his day's haul to procure the thing. It was strange; Thunder was such a bizarre being that it slipped their minds he had access to quite a sizable sum of money. The fisherman had been so ready to jump at the deal he'd even thrown in a few rods and the case of beer he'd brought along for the day. Thunder and Mano were making a sizable dent in the latter, Thunder purely by drinking and Mano by sipping and then pouring some over the side. Questioning had only gotten him to yield that it was an "island tradition" (he did it when he was on the island, so to Mano that counted) and nothing more.

Clint had bickered with his stowaway god for most of the night, the two seeming to discuss some pretty heavy issues. By the responses Clint made and the looks crossing his face, April suspected she was happier not being privy to Kodiwandae's side of the conversation. Most of them had slept in small spans of hours through the night, but as the morning rays broke across the ocean, only Clint was still slumbering. April didn't begrudge him that; if this was simply weird for the rest of them, it must be cusping on utter madness for Clint.

"Pretty surreal, huh?" Falcon crossed the ship and took a seat next to the younger woman.

"That's putting it mildly. You know I study biology, right? It's essentially the study of how everything works organically, mapping the complex system of life and how

132

that functions without things like magic or gods. Yet here I am, on a boat, during what was supposed to be my vacation, because a guy I've known for a couple of days is likely suffering a psychotic break." April expected the older hippie to tell her that she was rightly expanding her horizons, that she was opening up to all the things that existed beyond the scope of science and that doing so was a good thing.

"I hear that. If you'd have told me ten years ago I'd get an all-expenses paid vacation and wind up using it to try and restore an local deity, I'd have called you seventeen shades of stupid."

April knitted her eyebrows. "Really? I mean, this all sort of seems like, well… you've gone along with it fairly happily."

"We've all gone along with it, but if you remember, I'm the only one who needed a hands-on demonstration before I was even willing to leave the hotel room."

"I remember. I guess I assumed it was because you thought Clint was mocking the local culture, not because you didn't believe it was possible. No offense meant, but this whole thing does sort of seem in your comfort zone."

"None taken," Falcon said with a reassuring smile. "The ten-years-ago me and the me of today are very different people, obviously. I'm still not sure that I believe all of this: Kodiwandae being in Clint, the cat being king of the island, the pear being the only key to solve this whole mess. I mean, it's a lot to swallow."

"Yet here we are."

"Here we are. It's not because we're crazy, though, even if it turns out Clint just ate some bad pear and is having a very strange hallucination."

"That would excuse his delusion, but not ours."

Falcon patted April on her shoulder, the cotton t-shirt wrinkling under the weight of the older woman's hand. "There's nothing wrong with wanting to believe. Even if it leads down some unexpected roads, the desire itself is perfectly natural."

"Not to me."

"Oh? Well, perhaps you have gone daft then."

April shot Falcon a speculative glance, which the blue eyes that wrinkled at the corners returned with a strange confidence.

"Or maybe this is just scientific curiosity. Investigation of an anomaly in the accepted structure of the world."

"Also an excellent possibility," Falcon agreed.

"Land ho, bros!" Thunder's voice belted forth from the ship's front, where, sure enough, another island was visible on the horizon. Of course, it had been visible for several hours; it was just drawing close enough that departure was growing likely.

"I wonder how that one has been able to ride along on all this without showing so much as one instance of worry or doubt," April speculated.

"You could ask him, though I doubt either of us would understand the answer. They say children and idiots are the favorites of the gods, so maybe he just knows on some inner level that he is being looked after."

"Must be nice."

"Probably, but I find intellect a far better weapon than favor." Falcon's tone remained cheerful, but there was a flint of something that sparked inside her with those words. April might not be as good at reading people as she was at reading books, but even she could tell that beneath this peace and love mentality there was a basement of something more complex: a place that was shut away from the world, where armor and axes were carefully stowed and just beginning to rust.

"Chicas, you want some land brewskis?" Thunder called.

"Sure," Falcon said before April could object to the early hour. Thunder pitched the beers over with a technique that had been practiced and refined by manning the cooler

135

at countless parties. Falcon snatched both from the air and handed one to April.

"To searching." Falcon opened her beer and raised it in a toast. April hesitated then popped the top on the can in her hands.

"To intellect," April countered, raising her own drink.

"To intellect," Falcon agreed. The women clinked cans and sipped quietly as the boat drew closer to the island towering before them.

*   *   *

The Sahara, the Gobi, the very fires of hell had nothing on this parched patch of the world. The mere idea of water, the thought of moisture, was so foreign that the word itself would be choked away by dryness before it could ever be uttered. This cracked, craggy, desolate place was the sort of dry that could chug down a torrential flood and then five minutes later act as though there had never been a drop in the sky. Lucifer himself would have taken a stroll around, puffed out his chest, then made a very fast excuse about having left the iron on and departed. A torrent of cold water washed across the landscape, soothing and soaking, then vanished.

136

Kaia chugged the bottle of water, three empties already next to her hotel bed. Her throat still screamed for more, to the point where she contemplated rising from her bed and seeking out another bottle. Her first attempt at sitting up left her heaving the newly acquired water into the trashcan by her bed, so it was somewhat less than productive. She wiped her mouth with an unused pillow and flopped back down.

This was not a hangover. This was a punishment from the gods. She imagined she'd broken every commandment in every religion simultaneously to be cursed with this feeling. Honestly, she was just thankful she knew the hotel where she'd woken up. It was a quaint bed and breakfast on Alendola she'd often frequented in her more formative years.

Despite its reputation as a place to "get down and party", Alendola also housed an impressive library that specialized in local literature. Respected researchers from America frequently visited to comb its tomes, reveling in the sort of bibliophilic catacombs that academia had been invented for. Such places were rarer and rarer with the invention of the Internet, so it was of little surprise that a bright young Kaia Hale had met many travelers here while furthering her own thirst for knowledge, travelers with stories of the sweeping buildings and cold air that existed in other countries.

Of course, that was one very small draw on Alendola; most people knew it for its large parties and the hedonistic culture it marketed to tourists. It was a humorous incongruity that the same island could appeal to two vastly different groups, but out of form and ignorance (depending on the group), no one ever mentioned it.

Kaia stared at the slowly rotating ceiling fan, wishing she could remember exactly why she'd boarded the boat last night. It felt like she'd had a plan, a way to make it all feel better and resolve her nagging issues. That plan, if it had actually existed, belonged to Drunk Kaia, and Sober Kaia hadn't been included in the brainstorming session that conceived it. She supposed while she was here, the rational thing to do would be to probe the library to see what more she could learn about the Kodiwandae legend. It was one of the stories she'd put the least research into, seeing as even the faithful of Kenowai didn't really believe it. Who could trap a god, after all? That was before; now Kaia couldn't imagine why she hadn't put in countless hours reading over all the versions of the tale. Of course, that revelation had less to do with a new perspective on the anthropological implications of the story than it did with the golden pear she currently had stuffed in her backpack.

Kaia still didn't know why she'd taken it. Proof, probably; proof that she hadn't gone round the mental bend into Coo-Coo Town. She had looked at it a few times during the night: those moments stood out like flares along the dark highway of her drunken recollections. Sometimes she'd imagined (or possibly imagined that she was imagining) a feeling of energy coming from the fruit, like the sound one can hear when standing under power lines. Only in this case there were no such lines and it wasn't a sound. It was a feeling that echoed deep within her, in places Kaia had long forgotten existed.

All of that was subjective, however, dismissible by virtue of the whiskey or mere delusion. The pear's coloration was fact. Kenowai Pears grew light green on the vine then darkened to a hunter green when they were ready to be plucked. A hunter green pear had been what April set on the altar yesterday during the ceremony. After everything had happened, Kaia had noticed the pear was still whole and had snatched it before racing back to the bus. It had been her anchor in the sea of doubt. But while electricity could do many strange things, Kaia had never heard of a lighting strike changing a pear's color to gold. Not natural gold, either; this looked like someone had stoppered sunlight into a pear-shaped container.

Kaia didn't know what it meant; maybe nothing at all. Still, Kaia was a good scholar because she was obsessive, and she couldn't let go without an answer. She could walk away, certainly, but that wasn't the same as letting go. Walking away meant a lifetime of lying awake at strange hours of the night, of fleeting thoughts and theories assaulting her otherwise rational ideas. It meant the gnawing feeling in her gut, the one that kept telling her she was standing on the edge of some giant puzzle piece that could give shape to how the world works, would be with her forever. She couldn't bear that; one day of it had driven her to try and drink all the whiskey in Kenowai. A life of it would destroy her.

She tried to sit up, more slowly this time, and found while the room still spun, it eventually was willing to become stationary. Okay, she could move. Now where should she go? Water first; she felt like she could drain the ocean if it weren't so salty. Then a shower; no one should have to smell a girl detoxing this hard in the tropical heat with yesterday's funk piled on top. Once all that was attended to, Kaia could start her real endeavor: research.

Her wastebasket received a second helping from Kaia's stomach, but this time she didn't fall back into the comfort of the sheets. Dr. Kaia Hale had set her course with conviction and she would be damned if she let anything deter her from it. Aside from water and a shower, of course.

*   *   *

Alendola hosted a gorgeous city, glowing with a metropolitan charm entirely different from the rustic appeal of Kenowai. Kenowai had dirt roads, large wooden buildings, and ample space between everything for the animals to graze. The streets here were cobblestone paved, winding and weaving across the landscape as though the city's designer had been some layabout drunk. In truth, the designer had indeed been quite the booze hound, but he was certainly not a layabout. Lazy drunks didn't get elected to mayor and chief road planner.

The buildings were small stone creations that clustered together like children listening to ghost stories. Everywhere one looked there were signs of thriving life and commerce. To the foreigners, it was like a downtown section of some small town. To the people who lived on the islands, this was their New York or Chicago. Had it been on Kenowai, they might have jokingly called it The Big Pear. Instead most of the people here called it a sin-filled cesspit.

"Yeah, Big L, will do, keep it chill." Thunder's voice was slightly raised to be heard over the hearty wind that had developed a few minutes after they made landfall. Thunder turned off his mobile phone and slung it into his pocket. "Lawrence says for us to rockify up this town then slide home to Kenowai when we're done."

"I have a very hard time picturing him saying that," Clint disagreed.

"It's all in the tone, bro."

"At least he seemed to take it well," April said. After landing, it had finally dawned on them that perhaps the organizer of their little vacation might wonder what had happened to his charges when he found their rooms empty in the morning. So as they'd strolled the streets of Alendola, Thunder had made a quick call to bring him up to speed.

"Way más chipper than the ushe," Thunder concurred.

I think I'm missing something. I've scoured your language center over and over but I still can't completely understand what the one in the pink is saying.

"Um, yeah, that's due to… colloquial dialect," Clint said, tapping his forehead briefly. It was strange how quickly that had become second nature; he had to admit it kept things much clearer.

Really? Here I was beginning to suspect the man to be a moron.

Clint opened his mouth, but his stomach cut him off with a loud gurgle.

"I agree," Mano said to the noise. "We've been up all night and dinner was a long time ago; I think it is time to procure food."

"Agreed on the food; we also need to find a place to rest and recuperate. I don't know about you guys, but I'm reaching my limit for time spent in this kind of heat without a shower," April added.

"Shouldn't we stay on the trail, though? I mean, Kodiwandae did say it was tenuous at best," Falcon pointed out. She noticed a few heads turn and stare as she passed. As a woman who knew her looks and age down to the last wrinkle, she was under no illusions such stares were at her beauty. That left her words, which upon re-examination she realized could be taken as the ranting of a madwoman if someone were ill-informed of their situation.

"He did say that. I'm not sure if he has the same definition as tenuous that we do, though. I mean, if the cat could track it across open water, it's clearly not that flimsy." Clint tilted his head slightly, listening to the voice within. It had been disconcerting at first; however, the others were beginning to appreciate the habit. It at least told them he hadn't merely lapsed into his hitherto typical silence. "Also, it has been suggested we call our unseen friend Kodi for the time being. We're not exactly by ourselves anymore."

That they were not, as the full menagerie of Alendola's daytime occupants had burst forth from the surrounding stone buildings and were busy setting up stalls and loitering around, looking for tourists to con. Had the group not been walking with Mano, they would have been accosted by at least three "blind" beggars, two street performers who were actually distractions for thieves, and a member of the local clergy before they'd gotten half so far down this street. Luckily, it was an unwritten rule that friends of locals were not to be treated as rubes, so for the group it was actually a rather pleasant early morning walk.

"Good call; nothing wrong with a little discretion." April had also noticed the stares of the locals, but she'd picked up on a few the others had missed.

"In the meantime, what are we going to do? We need to eat, we have got to line up a hotel room or two, and we can't let the trail get cold," Clint summarized.

"Why not just do all three?" April proposed. "You and Mano keep up with the cat, Falcon and I will find a hotel and get some rooms, and Thunder can go grab food."

"How will you know where to find us if we split up?" Clint asked.

"You've got a cell phone, genius. The three of us can regroup at the fountain up ahead and then call and see where you're at. Do they have cabs on Alendola?"

"Many. The drivers are first-class cheats, but they are also excellent at getting you where you need to be," Mano informed her.

"Sounds like a good plan," Falcon said. "You two boys just make sure to go on foot; then when we've got everything taken care of we can grab a car over to wherever you've wound up."

"Word," Thunder, presumably, agreed.

"I guess it is the best use of our time," Clint said, reluctance heavy on his voice. He didn't know why, but something about this just rubbed him the wrong way. Maybe it was because it was too rational, a sound strategy in the midst of a mad adventure. He tried to brush the feeling aside; April was right, after all. Sooner or later they'd have to stop.

"All right, then, it's decided. Falcon and I will go talk to the hotels; Thunder, get something tasty and

144

portable since we'll have to bring it to Clint and Mano. When we're done, we meet at the fountain with the statue of the naked girl in the center."

"That's actually a statue of the goddess Alahai, frolicking amidst the waves," Mano informed her.

Clint, perhaps we should take a detour and go see this fountain up ahead.

"The cat is pointing the other way."

Well, yes, but it won't take but a minute. I really feel this is a chance to broaden your cultural horizons.

"When you're out of my body you can do what you want. For now, you'll just have to deal with a little disappointment."

"Sometimes I envy your position as divine transport," Falcon said. "Other times, I am quite thankful I wasn't the one the lighting struck."

"Believe me, if I knew how to trade I'd be all over it," Clint grumbled. "So, I guess we'll see you guys in a bit."

"Laters!" Thunder threw up a peace symbol and began jogging off down one of the winding side streets from which smoke and delicious smells were emanating, aided in range by the still powerful winds sweeping the island.

145

"You two be careful," April called as she and Falcon began heading down another road.

"Have fun!" Falcon urged.

Clint watched all three until they were gone from his sight. He had to fight the urge to yell for them to all come back. What was going on? He was never a worrier before and he didn't have any fresh reason to be now. Maybe the amount of shocks he'd had in such a short time was making him paranoid. Or, and this thought nearly made Clint chuckle out loud, what if this was more of Kodi's emotions bleeding through onto him? No, that was ridiculous. He needed to stop with the irrational fears and focus on real problems. Problems like finding the pear where a god's last scraps of power were tucked away.

"You okay?" Mano asked him. Clint realized he'd been standing there for several minutes now.

"Yeah, sorry. Just reflecting on how quickly the definition of 'normal' can change without it even being noticed, you know?"

"I sailed from my home in the middle of the night on the directions of a cat and a man with a god in his brain. I have an idea of what you mean."

"Good point. I guess we'd better get going."

The two set off in another direction, following the cat, who walked at the same steady pace as always. In all of

146

history there are few instances of truly powerful beings managing to hurry kings; but no one, not even the gods, can hurry a cat.

As they walked away, it was too bad they didn't look around a bit more, though it wouldn't have helped. Not even April's exceptional attention to detail would have picked out the concealed eyes charting their group's movements. Those eyes were hidden by years of skill and practice, and they would not be seen until they were good and ready. Which, based on the tourists' conversation, seemed like it wouldn't be too long at all.

13.

Lawrence stood on the bow of the ship and watched the crystal waters flow by. His journey was quite pleasant; the fierce winds blistering Alendola were nowhere to be seen in this vicinity. Unlike the others, he had taken the time to plan his journey a bit more, so rather than bartering or borrowing a fishing boat, Lawrence had booked private passage on a charter vessel that ran between the islands. There was excellent food, flowing champagne, and an air-conditioned cabin that functioned as a lounge. It was a far more pleasant experience, but it wasn't why he'd spent so much money to board it. The charter option offered something none of the others did: reliability. In the islands, a busted engine and rescheduling were easily written off as bad luck. Lawrence needed something that he could put more confidence in; he was running a tight timetable, after all.

A man with less experience might have patted his pocket or nudge the bag by his feet to make sure the essential equipment he'd spent the morning gathering was still there. Lawrence had no such need. He could feel the weight in his breast pocket and the pressure on his ankle where the respective loads rested. No nimble pickpocket had slipped away with his goods and soured his plans. Everything was going as expected.

As he watched a dolphin begin leaping alongside the boat, Lawrence noted that traditionally this was where most people's plots began to unravel. The others on the boat, wealthy enough to be here but still simple enough to care about a jumping mammal, rushed to the side and pointed at it. Some commenced with snapping a flurry of pictures that would be blurry at best yet would still wind up as the centerpiece on a miserable mantelpiece.

Lawrence stepped away from the crowd and headed into the cabin. He might treat himself to a crab cake or two. No champagne, of course. Lawrence might be confident in the events he'd set in place; however, he was not one to tempt fate. A moment's lapse in judgment could bring the world tumbling down. That was why Lawrence's plans didn't unravel: he never took success for granted. Lawrence was alert to the possibility that he would need to do damage control every minute. Though, in this circumstance, he felt the odds were relatively low.

The air conditioning struck Lawrence in the face as he stepped through the doors. A tall man in a white shirt held out a tray for him. On it appeared to be meatballs with a gooey sauce. There was certainly some fancy culinary term for them; just as certainly as they would still taste like meatballs with gooey sauce.

"Thank you." Lawrence took a toothpick and speared a few. Might as well enjoy himself. He ambled over to a leather couch and settled down. He wondered if he would still enjoy little pleasures like this once everything was over. He expected he would, or he'd find new ones to take their place. Lawrence was a man of excellent determination; if he had to search high and low to

149

find entertainment that is exactly what he would do. That was in the future, though; he had to concern himself with the now. Everything came down to those Goodwin brothers. Between the cocky quiet one and the loud idiot, Lawrence was confident they'd accomplish their task. And if not... well, Lawrence had a backup plan or ten.

One bite of the meatballs was more than enough, and Lawrence discreetly hid the rest in his napkin and tucked it away in a wastebasket. No reason to be rude to the chef.

* * *

April and Falcon had finished up the arrangements for the hotel in far less time than expected. They took their time walking back, enjoying the sights of the city as they ambled along the winding streets. It was relaxing, easy, and they could almost pretend they were still on a normal vacation. April paused and bought a small handbag from a local vendor. She wasn't sure why, but its festive and frivolous nature had called to her for some reason. Falcon resisted such impulse purchases, although she did enjoy watching the vendors hawk their wares using spirited enthusiasm (lies).

"I've been meaning to ask you something," April said as they passed by a small man aggressively claiming his goat stew would cure any ailment and win the love of any woman. "When Kodi read you, he said your name wasn't really Falcon Rainwater. Why did you lie?"

"I didn't. A name is something you choose to go by more than anything else. I left my old life and my old name behind, so to me, Falcon is my real name."

"Oh. Why?"

"You aren't a terribly socially adept girl, are you?"

"I've been told that before, so I'm forced to think there is some truth to it."

"At least you're aware." Falcon sighed. "For reference, it is considered bad form to ask someone about a past they've clearly worked hard to put behind them. To give you the rough overview of it, I used to be less in touch with the world around me. Then some things happened that made me see that I needed more in my life. Since then I've devoted myself to the goddess of the earth and the balance in the world she represents."

"That was quite rough."

"I warned you."

The two women walked on for a bit in silence, April analyzing and cataloguing what the older woman had said, Falcon wondering what strange karma she had acquired to set her life on a path with these people in it. Before they noticed, they'd walked long enough to arrive at the fountain of Alahai. They looked around briefly, but neither was surprised to find they'd beaten Thunder. Difficulty of jobs aside, he could be a bit unfocused even on the best of days. Luckily, there were some stone benches around the fountain where they could rest.

"I have another question for you; however, it might be unintentionally rude."

"I'm adequately braced," Falcon assured her.

"If we do find this pear, or a pear that Clint says is the right one, and we go to the next island and do everything we have to do, what are you hoping will happen?"

"Obviously I hope it works and Kodi is restored to his former glory."

"Really? I keep going over the possibilities in my head and that actually seems like one of the worst ones."

"Because we'll have earned the gratitude of a divine being?"

"Because there is such thing as a divine being: something metaphysical, something beyond science and ration. If a god actually leaps out of Clint's head, it means everything I've studied, everything I've planned to build my entire life on, is pointless. Why bother with science when you're burdened with the knowledge that the world has magic?"

"You know, there is an old quote about magic just being science we don't understand yet."

"I've heard it. We used to laugh about it in our advanced chemistry classes."

"Think of it this way then: even if there are gods and magic, that doesn't mean science doesn't have its place. Cars, planes, electricity, medicine, computers, and countless other things are all the byproducts of people like you, April. Gods didn't make them, and they certainly don't run on wishes or fairy dust. Science still makes our lives better. All that magic does is provide a spark of hope when all the rational options have run out."

"That does make a certain amount of sense." April knit her eyebrows together in concentration as she integrated Falcon's principles into her world view. The hippie smiled to herself. Maybe all those years in law weren't such a waste if she could use her super arguing powers for good.

Falcon was only able to bask in the satisfaction of a job well done for a few seconds before both women's attention was torn elsewhere.

A lean local in a Yankees ball cap raced by them, his dexterous arm snapping out and ripping April's festive new bag right out of her lap.

"Hey!" April leapt to her feet and dashed after him, her long legs trimming the distance almost immediately. April might be a nerd, but she was a biology nerd. As such, she understood the importance of a good diet and cardio, which culminated in her being a practiced runner. Falcon trailed behind them, her own physique not quite on par with the younger woman's.

The man zigged and zagged between other pedestrians, never shaking his pursuers entirely but not getting out of range of them, either. Later on, April would look back at this and chastise herself for not noticing the careful way he paced his movements. In that moment, however, all she saw was his sprinting form, and she kept after him like she'd popped a GPS in his shoes. Eventually he moved off the main street, ducking onto a side path that wound through the buildings. April took the turn without a second thought, her own heart pumping hard with adrenaline and determination as she rocketed after that thieving asshole.

She'd no sooner gone around the corner than she felt a pair of strong hands seize her neck and drive her to the brick wall. Her own momentum did most of the damage, crashing her torso against the unyielding material and driving the wind from her lungs. Her arms were grabbed and pinned before she could recover.

"Nothing personal, lady," the voice half growled and half whispered in her ear. She wanted to yell but she still hadn't gotten her breath back, so it merely came out as ragged gasps. "The boss just noticed you folks were

154

dressed pretty nicely and not being too careful about showing off your money. So we'll take everything you've got and be on our way."

April might have felt relieved if not for the way his voice thickened on the word "everything." The adrenaline that had been pumping thanks to rage was now coursing due to fear. Just like that, she'd gone from a sunny bench by a fountain to a shadowed alleyway down a side road.

Falcon's silhouette appeared in the alley's entrance, and for a fleeting moment April felt hope. Then she noticed the two figures walking alongside her and realized the older woman was in the same position as she.

"Sorry," April wheezed out from her minimal air supply.

Falcon smiled at her reassuringly. "We walk with gods, child. Everything will be fine."

April had never believed in anything that couldn't be tested and re-tested to prove hypothesis, but she nodded to the vulnerable old hippie anyway. Given how bad things could go, this hardly seemed like the time to be taking away someone else's hope.

*   *   *

"You okay?"

Clint shook his head and focused. His mind kept ambling off in its own direction; he couldn't stay focused. He realized he'd been standing in the same spot for nearly a minute, just staring at the street. No wonder Mano was concerned.

"I'm fine, I think. Just can't shake this nagging worry."

Worry?

"Worry?"

"Yeah, like something bad is going to happen. It's strange; I'm not usually the pessimistic type, but today the feeling keeps hounding me."

"Given the last day or so you've had, I can see being a little worried about bad things happening," Mano said, patting him on the shoulder reassuringly. "If we don't keep up with the king that prediction might come true, though."

"You're right. Let's go." The two men began jogging after Sprinkles, who hadn't even entertained the idea of breaking his gait for the humans following him.

When did you first get this feeling?

"Back when we were splitting up. I'm probably just feeling weird because we've been clustered together since this first happened."

Would that be a normal experience for you?

"Well... no. Then again, who knows what normal is anymore. Why?"

Just curious. Trying to get a better understanding of you mortals while I've got the opportunity.

Clint accepted the lie and continued the feline pursuit. Kodiwandae, on the other hand, was left with something of a puzzle. His host seemed to be experiencing slight premonitions of upcoming events. Very few humans had this gift, and of those who did, most dismissed it as exceptional intuition. Clint clearly didn't have it; Kodiwandae had scoured his memories when they first met and not come across any previous instances of such a thing. Mortals didn't just develop such skills all of a sudden, either; it was the sort of thing you were born with or you weren't. Gods were different. Every god could feel the way events would begin to pull one way or another. This didn't apply to their own circumstances, but it was as dependable as a sunrise when looking at the lives of mortals.

This left one completely implausible explanation: Kodiwandae's power, the power he didn't even have, was beginning to leak into Clint. It didn't make a lick of sense, though. Then again, Kodiwandae had found very little about his host that made sense. Mortals were, in his

157

experience, defined by their Wants. Not by mere necessities, but by the big desires that filled them up and drove them forward. It was their Wants that let them persevere through impossible odds and achieve greatness.

The Wants of mortals were what defined gods, too; after all, they were what the humans prayed for. Those were the things that gods could grant to increase someone's Belief. Or, if the wrong Want was granted, destroy it. It was the reason Kodiwandae had planted that damn pear tree: the people had Wanted a new source of fruit on the island that didn't taste like three-day-old goat. Wants gave shape and power to many things, yet for the first time, Kodiwandae had found someone without any. Clint's brain was empty of such things, suffocated and smothered under a half-assed philosophy and a memory of bloody greasepaint. It was like Kodiwandae was a cup of water dropped into the ground; without any desires to give him shape he was formless, running all over the place.

Clint huffed along as they left the merchant district and entered a more upscale area. The buildings were larger and some of them even had signs designating them as legitimate businesses. Kodiwandae saw all the sights secondhand, watching them filter through Clint's eyes and into the storage section of his brain. Maybe the formlessness was why Clint was getting a premonition; without distinct lines between the two of them, it was easy for the edges to get a bit blurry. No, that still didn't make sense. Kodiwandae didn't have any power without the pear; Nature had been quite thorough in separating him from his realm. Even if Clint was getting some of Kodiwandae's

158

essence, he shouldn't be able to use it; it wasn't like there was some free-floating power source out there for him to… to…

I'm a fucking idiot.

"Why do you say that?"

If Kodiwandae could have blinked, he would have. He didn't mean to say that last part out loud, or whatever qualified as "out loud" in this situation. He really was losing a grip on himself.

Nothing, just remembered something I'd forgotten.

"Anything that will-" Clint's words died off as a new wave of terror washed over him. He couldn't even move; he doubled over and fought to keep standing. This wasn't normal. This wasn't just some nagging doubt. Clint felt like he was stuck in a horror movie, every sound a new monster coming to tear the flesh from his bones. In that moment he knew, He Knew, something awful either had or was about to happen.

"What… is this?"

"What happened? You sick?" Mano jogged back over to him.

It's a premonition.

"What?"

A sense of something that is going to come before it does.

"But how?"

I've got a theory, but it might take a while to explain.

"You're getting pale." Mano slipped his arm around Clint's shoulders and began moving him out of the street. "Let's get you into a place with air conditioning. There's a library a few blocks up the road."

"Wait, what should I do? What's going to happen?"

No idea. That's the bitch of premonitions; they're usually just feelings without any instructions. All you can do is sit back and hope you're in the right place to make a difference when it happens.

"That kind of sucks."

"Talk to Kodi inside," Mano urged him. "Right now we need to get you off the street."

Clint bit back his questions and tried to rise above his sense of fear. He managed to make it four steps before leaning against the side of a building and dry-heaving. Mano was right; they couldn't stay here. Clint set his resolve and began lumbering forward with all the speed he could muster.

14.

April was surprised at how organized the gang was. Two others had appeared from the either side of the alley, bringing the total to five. April thought one of them looked a touch familiar then realized he'd been near the stall where she bought the purse. That sort of explained it; she hadn't been as covert as she should have been about all the extra cash she was carrying around, cash she'd brought for incidentals on what was supposed to be her nice, relaxing vacation. Likely they hung out looking for people with more money than safety sense and struck when the targets were vulnerable. April would have never been so careless in normal circumstances. All this… this stupid nonsense had gotten her addled. How was a girl supposed to keep real dangers in mind when she was struggling with the possibility of discovering her entire view of the universe was askew?

Falcon, for her part, didn't bother blaming herself or their muddled circumstances. She blamed the people who were currently robbing them. If she were a few years younger, she might show them exactly what Valerie Quinn did to people who wronged her. That was a big 'if', though, since she wasn't a few years younger and Valerie Quinn wasn't here. No, there was only Falcon Rainwater, and Falcon Rainwater had only one real avenue of recourse in this situation: she prayed. There was no head bowing or mumbled words; Falcon simply cast her hope into the universe like an avian enthusiast tossing seeds to the wind.

She recognized the odds of them being answered were slender, but that was the point: a spark of hope when all rational options had run out.

"So what do we do with them now?" One of the smaller ones was talking to the man they thought of as Runner, the thief who'd snatched April's purse.

"We don't need the old one anymore." Well, that was going to do wonders for Falcon's already-waning self-confidence. "As for the dark one, I think we can-"

"Thundeeeeer PUNCH!"

All eyes turned to the blur of pink polo that was barreling down the alley, intention clearly set on Runner. Thunder's arm was cocked back and he didn't even try to slow down as he drew near. Instead he incorporated the momentum into the assault, putting every last bit of power he could muster in the right hook he hurled at Runner.

Of course, given that he had announced his presence and telegraphed his attack, it should hardly come as a surprise that Runner moved fluidly to the side of Thunder's punch, grabbing the newcomer by the back of his frosted-haired head and slamming it into the brick wall. Thunder collapsed like a rag doll, a trickle of blood running down from his forehead behind the aviator glasses.

"Thunder!" April yelled, struggling to get free and run over to him. He might be, well, okay, he obviously *was* an idiot, but he'd rushed in to help without a second thought. The idea that he could be seriously injured was something April found herself suddenly unable to tolerate. Sadly, her captor didn't share such sentiments, so all April succeeded in doing was injuring her arm as she fought against his superior muscle and leverage.

"Young man, I don't know if you're the religious type, but I have a piece of advice for you. You should pray very hard that our friend is not badly hurt." Falcon's voice was calm, but everyone in an audible range felt a prickle run up the back of his or her spine. Lawrence would have been both impressed and supremely attracted to her in that moment.

"Sorry, old lady, I'm not afraid of your little friend or of some withered old gods." Runner flashed a smirk that Falcon would have traded half her remaining years to smack off of him.

"There are scarier things in this world than gods, young man."

"Though I like to think we do in a pinch."

Clint walked slowly down the alley, his eyes even but his expression scowling. It was the first time Falcon could remember his face matching the tone of Kodiwandae's voice when it came from his mouth. And for some inexplicable reason it was that thought, that realization, which got Falcon over the hill of doubt she'd been climbing for ten years. In that moment, she Believed.

"You'll suffice," was all she said aloud.

*   *   *

Kaia flipped through another book, making notes on a yellow legal pad as she read. This was the fourth retelling of the story of Kodiwandae she'd uncovered so far. If the pile of books surrounding her was any indication, this would not be the last one she found. Kaia was beating back her hangover the same way she had in college: by swelling her brain full of so much information the headache had no room to take root. Of course, the aspirin and five additional bottles of water she'd downed before leaving the hotel had also proven to be quite helpful.

She wasn't the only person in the library that day, but she was one of the few. Despite its strong academic reputation, there wasn't much call for such places on a regular basis. When people with fancy credentials weren't deigning to visit this book refuge it went largely underutilized by the local population. This worked just fine for Kaia and the other nerds; it allowed one the freedom and space to work with little risk of distraction.

The only sound to pierce the study-filled silence was the opening of the library's main doors. They were vast wooden slabs that stood just beyond the archaic circulation desk, and the act of pulling them ajar took either

164

great strength or great dedication. They blasted the room with light and heat when one was successful in budging them open, but an experienced bookworm could learn to ignore even that grand event with honed selective attention.

It was for that reason that Kaia didn't even look up when a pair of figures entered the library. She was absorbed in this new version of Kodiwandae's story. The first section was still the same as what she knew; however, it seemed that the oral version had segmented off part of the legend over time. This book's version said that the goddess had not just sealed away Kodiwandae in his tree, she had also severed him from the realm where he drew his power so he wouldn't be able to free himself. This act was not malicious, merely logistical. The goddess had promised to fully restore Kodiwandae once he was free and he called to her from her temple. She'd even put the power he'd had at the time into the air about the tree, assuring him it would be condensed by the same ceremony that would set him free.

Kaia reached down and touched her backpack. If there was a more fitting vessel for Kodiwandae's power than the pear used to free him, she couldn't think of it. It would certainly explain the strange golden color at least. Then again, when your explanation involved accepting mythology as fact, it was hardly a Grade-A option. Kaia knew what she'd seen, though. It didn't matter if she actually believed the stories or not; this was where the evidence was pointing. Facts weren't true because you thought they were right: they were true because they were true.

She checked the author of the book and rose from her seat to go see if he had any more works on the shelves. She turned from the table and found herself looking into two sets of recently familiar eyes.

"My, what a coincidence running into you," Justin said. He smiled at her, but Kaia noticed the way Dustin repositioned himself to block the nearest avenue of exit.

"Small world, I guess. What brings you two here?"

"We were just touring the islands now that our work is done. Seeing the local sights, you know."

"Right. Well, be sure to check out the cherry tree forest. It should be blooming nicely this time of year."

"I'm sure we will. At the moment we're feeling a bit hungry, however; all the touring can work up quite an appetite. You don't happen to have one of those Kenowai Pears on you, perchance? That would be simply... divine."

Creepy and with little grasp of subtlety, Justin had all the makings of a great ex-boyfriend. She didn't know how they'd found out about the pear or knew that she had it, but playing dumb clearly wasn't even on the table. Justin was staring at her patiently while Dustin kept glancing over his shoulder to see if anyone was paying attention. They weren't and they wouldn't start any time soon. It seemed her options were quite limited.

"I've got the one from the altar yesterday. Something about the lightning messed with its coloration so I wanted to examine it. It's actually pretty intriguing, want to see?"

"I'd love to." Justin tensed as she reached into her backpack, ready for her to throw it in his face and make a break for it or some such idiocy. Instead her hand emerged with a pear that was indeed very strange-looking. One moment it seemed to be glowing, then the next he was sure it had just been a trick of the light, and then he'd flip-flop again.

"You need to hold it to really appreciate the curiousness. It's almost like there's a current running through it." Kaia held out the pear, her eyes gleaming with intellectual passion.

Justin accepted it from her and thought to himself that for some girl with a Ph.D., she certainly wasn't all that swift. Personally, if he'd been in her situation, he'd at least have tried something to hold on to this little chunk of the arcane. Maybe she really didn't know what she had; he supposed it was possible.

"It certainly does seem to lo-GAAAAAH!"

Justin's scream shredded the library's sacred silence as Kaia whipped her now-free hand out of her bag and pepper-sprayed him in the eyes. Dustin rushed forward to help and got his own helping of mace for the trouble.

"You bitch!" Dustin began rubbing his eyes furiously; Justin was already too far gone to retain any sight. As he tried his damnedest to wipe away the chemical contagion, he realized at some point the pear had left his possession.

"I spent four years living in New York, you stupid fucks; you think I don't know how to deal with thugs?"

Kaia hurriedly stuffed her mace and the pear back into her bag. She began to dash down the aisle, then paused and grabbed the book she'd been reading from the table. She threw that in the bag too and began making her escape. Other people were gathering at her section: even in a place as isolationally-minded as this, screaming and chemical attacks were going to draw interest.

"Sexual assault!" Kaia yelled as she dashed. "Those two foreigners tried to grab my breasts!" The glances that had once been speculative began to harden. Nobody doubted that off-islanders were morally bankrupt devils that would happily prey on defenseless damsels. To do it to one of their women, though, and here in a sanctum of education during the middle of the day, that was spitting in the face of the entire community.

Justin's vision began to return and he immediately wished it hadn't. The other people in the library were forming a tightening circle around them, the expressions on their faces leaving no question as to whether they believed Kaia's outlandish claims. Justin was confident he could handle a couple of them, but there were more than a couple,

168

and some had the looks, muscles, and tattoos of men who had once possessed less-peaceful interests before discovering the joy of literature.

"What's going on?" Dustin asked.

"It is entirely possible that we might be in deep shit," his brother replied. He couldn't be sure due to his still-addled sight, but he was fairly certain he saw one of the larger people in the crowd, a dark-haired man with large shoulders and a tattoo of a shark on his neck, nod in agreement with his assessment. This did not bode well.

15.

Clint took in the scene before him. Falcon and April being restrained by burly men, Thunder lying on the ground with a trickle of blood running down his forehead, and three ruffians unencumbered and readying themselves to deal with this new minor threat. He felt something blooming inside his chest, a rush that seemed to fire through his blood and brain. All of a sudden his ears began to ring and his skull began to throb. It was anger surging through him, but a fiercer version of it than he'd ever experienced. This wasn't just anger at some slight wrong or perceived injustice. This was the righteous rage of one who sees the innocent being hurt.

"I hope this works," Clint mumbled under his breath.

Me, too. You're sure you want to go through with it? There's a lot of risk.

The blood from Thunder's head was flowing down between the lenses of his aviators. Clint couldn't tell if his friend was breathing anymore. He wasn't sure when these people had become more than just traveling companions to him; maybe it was during the ceremony, or on the hill, or in the boat, but it had happened. They were his friends, whether he meant for them to be or not. Clint tightened his fist and his resolve. He didn't answer Kodiwandae verbally. He didn't need to; even if Kodiwandae couldn't sense precise thoughts, there was no mistaking an intention that powerful building in the brain.

Clint's skin began to tingle, a sensation altogether different from the blood rush he'd just experienced. This felt different, smoother, like some piece of him he'd never noticed was expanding. Kodiwandae began to form a word in Clint's throat. Clint had never been more aware of the tremors of his vocal chords: each vibration sent ripples of burning heat through his throat. As the word rose toward his mouth, Clint would have sworn he was vomiting a cinder. It hurt unlike anything he'd ever experienced, but he didn't try to cry out or tell Kodiwandae to stop. This was happening, for better or worse. As Clint opened his mouth to let the word escape, he was almost surprised when the sound reached his ears. He'd have sworn such a word would scorch the very air.

"RUN."

There was a moment where the world seemed to slip a bit, a disoriented drunk momentarily losing its cosmic footing. Then everything righted itself and the thugs were dashing down the alleyway with a gusto one wouldn't have imagined their slinking sullen forms could muster. April, Falcon, and heaven-only-knew-who-else's things fell from their arms and pockets as they dashed, their legs pumping, their feet slamming the ground as though it had done them some great wrong. They disappeared in mere seconds but they kept on running for a very long time before they slowed and even then it would be quite some while before any of them ever felt truly safe.

Falcon rubbed her arms and stared at the young man who had so easily dispersed the villains. If not for Kodi's voice, she didn't think she would have recognized him as the same slacker she'd first met in the Camelot Burgers conference room only days ago. Part of the transformation was the way he held himself: his sullen slump had been replaced with the demeanor of a king walking among his subjects. Another part was the hard, outlined conviction that he wore across his face. Of course, the most noticeable part was probably the fact that his eyes were glowing with golden light, though that was slowly fading.

April didn't notice anything besides the eyes, partially because she wasn't as adept at reading people as Falcon and partially because she'd rushed to Thunder as soon as she was free. She took his pulse, opened his eyelids, and tested his breathing in rapid succession.

"I think he's okay," April said with evident relief. "But we should still get him to a hospital to be professionally checked out. It should be okay to move him."

"We'll get him there," Falcon said. "Though it would be easier if the muscular boy were here. I don't suppose you brought Mano with you?"

Clint shook his head. "I told him to keep up with the cat and gave him my cell phone so we could call when we were done. Let's get Thunder to a doctor." He stooped down and slipped an arm around Thunder's shoulder, hoisting him to his feet while supporting his weight. April immediately flanked Thunder on the opposite side; the duo soon found they could haul their cargo around without too much strain if they kept the weight distributed between them.

They began moving down the alley slowly, making sure each had a firm grip as they progressed, fearful of losing their hold and doing more damage. Falcon walked alongside them, steadying anyone who looked a touch unstable. To her credit, they made it out of the alley before Falcon's curiosity got the better of her.

"So, are you going to explain what happened back there? That seemed like more than just a terrifying voice, it felt like divine intervention. I thought Kodi couldn't do anything without the pear?"

"He can't. I can, though."

"It's a bit complicated."

"Try anyway."

"Let's say that Belief and Wants are what give Kodi his abilities. Normally, he would draw that power from the realm he occupies, you know, from people who specifically Believe in him."

"Like prayers?"

"Close enough for now. Anyway, not all Belief is directed. Some people put their faith in more general things, like positive thinking toward their goals or just hoping there is something indefinable out there. That stuff permeates the world; it's a blank slate. It can be anything the user wants it to be."

"What was it today?" April asked.

"*A gentle nudge. You can give them to reality if you know how. I used it to suggest that those rogues really wanted to be running instead of mugging.*"

"Pretty useful," Falcon said.

"No kidding," Clint agreed. "He says it's what people with divine blood use to get their special abilities. Since I'm human and connected to the world, I can interact with it. It's kind of like he uses me to draw the Belief in, then he can mold it as needed."

"So it's a team effort," April summed up. "That might have come in handy a few times on our little trip, by the way."

"*I wasn't aware the human could make use of such ambient energy until he began experiencing a premonition.*"

"You what?" Falcon kept her voice from growing to a yelp, but not without some effort.

"Yeah, it's why I showed up. I kept getting these bursts of terror about someone being hurt. I ran back to the fountain and then-"

Falcon's phone began chirping an awful tune, interrupting Clint's explanation. She pulled it from her purse and saw it was Clint's number, which meant Mano was calling. She popped it open immediately.

"Hello, Mano… Yes, yes he told me… Uh-huh… Oh dear, you're sure? No, I believe you… We're taking Thunder to the hospital right now… Yes… We think he's fine. It's a long story… Okay, we'll go to that one and meet you there." She flipped the phone shut briskly and stowed it back in her pocket. "That was Mano; he is going to meet us at the hospital."

"What about the cat?" Clint asked.

"That was why he called. A few minutes ago it stopped walking. It looked around for a bit, then sat on its haunches and stared at him. He thinks it lost the trail."

"*Uh-oh.*"

"What uh-oh?"

"*I did tell you there were risks.*"

"Why would my thing affect the cat?"

"We dropped a mystical depth charge on the area. The trail of the pear has been weak from the beginning; that much power probably blasted away all the residual energy there was to follow."

"So, what now?"

"Now we get Thunder some help," April interrupted. "It sounds like our current lead has gone cold anyway, so let's use the time to regroup and think of something."

"You're a curiously apt woman."

"Flattery later, lifting now."

The four progressed as such down the road, drawing many curious glances from passers-by. Elsewhere on the island, five rogue youths continued to sprint with a fervor that would have made Kenyan Olympians jealous.

*　　*　　*

Kaia almost made it out of her hotel safely. She dashed there from the library, books clutched in hand and breath panting from her mouth, to grab a few pieces of jewelry she'd been wearing last night and had known Alendola well enough to lock in the room safe this morning. She reasoned that she would be fine. They didn't know where she was staying, and even if they did, there was no way they could slip away fast enough to intercept her. The islanders might put up with a lot, but their compassion for people who came after their women was legendarily nonexistent.

That's probably why she was more concerned with determining her next move instead of scanning for familiar presences as she bounded out the lobby after checking out. She was so absorbed in the implication of what it could all mean if this pear really did hold the abilities of a god that she didn't see the figure stealthily creeping up behind her.

She did, however, feel the sharp prick of a blade being pressed between her shoulders at the same time as a rough hand found rest upon her shoulder.

"Walk to the bathroom." There was no room for argument in Justin's voice; he clearly hadn't taken the pepper spray thing so well.

Kaia obliged, altering her course toward the nearest lavatory. She wanted to go to the men's and pray some strapping fellow with knife-breaking magic was conveniently taking a piss, but Justin steered her toward the ladies. As soon as they were through, Kaia felt him rip her bag from her shoulder and shove her forward. She landed hard, the audible crack from her wrist informing her she was injured before the pain could travel up the nervous system.

"I'm amazed you got away so quickly."

"Dustin has his issues, but he is malleable. He dealt with the crowd while I slipped away."

"You ran out on your own brother. I knew you guys were creepy but I thought you'd at least be loyal."

"I am exceptionally loyal," Justin said as he rooted though the bag, "which is why I never lose sight of the job. Especially the one that will pay for all of our busted equipment from your damn ceremony." He pulled out the pear triumphantly then threw her bag over a stall door.

"How did you even know about the pear? I didn't know what it was until an hour ago."

"I might be more inclined to tell you had you not maced Dustin and me earlier. As it is, just be thankful I don't have time to return the favor."

Kaia sneered up at him with all the defiance she could muster. "I don't know what you think you know, but it doesn't matter who finishes the ceremony. There's no reward to it for anyone besides Kodiwandae."

"Finish the ceremony? Dear girl, you are mistaken. We've been contracted to ensure this little adventure goes uncompleted for as long as possible." With that, Justin exited slowly, his eyes never leaving the fallen woman's form.

She waited until she was sure he was gone then tested her wrist. Definite sprain, possibly a break. She'd have to go to a doctor. Kaia was experienced enough to know that a good setting would take care of the injury in a few weeks. The hole she was feeling in her gut, though, the pear-shaped one that had briefly held the ember of excitement over discovering something beyond her, that would take substantially longer to heal.

16.

April and Thunder were in the small doctor's office, Thunder sitting on the table with an icepack held to his head and April pacing the room while chewing on a strand of her hair.

"What is taking so long? He already got the X-rays, reading them shouldn't be this hard."

"Chillax, el cabesa de Thunder has taken hits way más awesome than that."

"I can't just 'chillax'; you could be seriously injured."

"Nah, my gooey thought lump is just a little extra gooey."

"You can't possibly know that. You were out for several minutes. There could be brain damage, or a concussion, or a subdural hematoma, or a hundred other things wrong!"

"Just a noggin bump and eventually a bitchin' scar."

"How can you be so unconcerned? This is your brain we're talking about."

"You've got a good rile of worry on. That making you more soothed?" Thunder adjusted the ice pack to a different section of his throbbing skull.

"Well… no."

"My way's got me hanging on a smooth chill. Why fix what ain't broke? Like my bro Squishins used to say, 'Worry is the nemesis of productive thought. One must first decide that the tasks before them can be surmounted, and then the mind's only preoccupation should be with devising the methodology to accomplish such a task'. Or something like that."

April stared at him, his polo and shorts now dirty from lying in the street, half the side of his frosted tips matted with blood, and an unflappable smile slapped across his face. "One of your bros said all that?"

"Yeah, Squishins could go off the deep end when he had the right mix of Jäger and Kahlua running through him."

"Uh-huh." April didn't quite believe him; however, she didn't see any productive result in arguing the point. Instead, she quit pacing and hopped onto the table next to him. "I, um, I don't know if I've said it yet, but thank you."

"For getting a classic lesson in ass-stompage? No worries."

"For running in the way you did to help us. Even you had to have noticed there were more people than you could have possibly handled, but you still ran in full force. That was sweet."

"Nah, you're my girl-bros. They go for you, they gotta deal with the Thunder."

April snorted a laugh in spite of herself. "I keep meaning to ask: the first day you said we could call you Thunder for short. What's your full name?"

"Fuckin' Sexual Thunder."

"I… okay, I actually meant your full real name, not your nickname, but wow, now I want to know the story behind that."

Thunder shifted his icepack again. "Well, the realio dealio nameio is buried in the brain vault, but I would be glad to tell you the story of how Fuckin' Sexual Thunder shattered onto the world and began to wreck it with awesomeness."

April started to object then realized it was either this or going back to pacing the floors. Though Thunder might be a strange and curious person, he was able to take her mind off the worrying. That was something very few things had ever done for April and she wasn't inclined to get off this odd ride just yet.

"I'd like that. Go ahead."

*   *   *

The mood in the waiting room was considerably less cheerful. Sprinkles sat on a green plastic seat, licking his paws to try and get the foreign dirt out of his fur. He'd been making solid progress toward his target: in fact, he was almost positive he'd nearly reached it, but the ripple that spread through the city had purged the ethereal trail into nothingness, leaving nothing to rely on but sheer intuition. Sprinkles' gut had told him it was time to regroup, so he'd forsaken the search and waited for the humans to come back together. They hadn't taken long; his subject used the hand phone to call the others, and they met in a place that smelled of disinfectant and fear. Sprinkles was not partial to either of these scents; however, he waited patiently while the loud one was ushered behind some doors and the dark one went with him. These people had incurred wounds while on a grand quest for the Kingdom of Kenowai; Sprinkles could show such injuries the proper deference while they were treated.

"That sounds pretty amazing; I wish I could have seen it," Mano said. Falcon had just described the bit of magic Clint had pulled in the alleyway, perhaps adding some additional flair for story-telling purposes.

"It was pretty spectacular," Falcon agreed. "I just wish it hadn't come with such a hefty price."

"It is strange to think we've come so far in the past day only to lose the trail completely. Now what do we do?" Mano seemed to be losing his accent more and more the longer he hung out with the group.

"I don't know. Hopefully Clint and Kodi will come up with something," Falcon said.

The duo that was a solo had been sitting off in a corner by themselves for the past several minutes. Clint didn't seem to be talking much, his face remaining uncharacteristically pinched in concern. Whether it was worry over Thunder or fear that he had lost his only path to freedom, Falcon could have never guessed. In fact, both were weighing on his mind, but there was something more prevalent causing his facial anomaly.

"I don't know how to explain it, something just feels different," Clint muttered under his breath. He realized anyone looking at him would assume he had arrived (too late) for mental treatment. He didn't really care at this particular moment. "Like, if the entirety of who I am was a written paragraph, and someone took that paragraph and ran it through an Internet translator into Russian, then ran it through again to make it English. Things would more or less still add up, but there would be parts that were off, not the same as they used to be."

I warned you there would be risks.

"I know. Just, can you help me understand why I suddenly feel like, I don't know, like bits of me are askew?"

It was impossible to put into words no matter how he tried. Physically, Clint felt the same; mentally, he was still intact; and emotionally, he seemed about as stable as always. Yet somewhere in the core of his being he knew some part of him had shifted a bit in one direction: a single hair out of place on the head of his metaphorical soul.

Humans aren't meant to touch that kind of power; they have their own sources for magic. There's a reason only those with divine heritage can utilize it. I don't really know what the side effects are, or what they might be long term. No one has ever done this before. Kodiwandae was actually surprised that Clint had noticed such a subtle difference so quickly. This guy had a very strong sense of self.

"So it might be nothing?"

Right. Maybe it's just a metaphysical electrical shock. Instead of feeling all twitchy you feel like this.

"I think I'm going to choose to believe that." It was the best approach, really. Why worry about some nagging feeling that even a god couldn't explain when he had no way of fixing it? Besides, even if it was something that would unravel his very being, it was on him. Kodi had adamantly warned him that something like this was dangerous, but he'd accepted that responsibility to help the others. He'd do it again, too.

Probably for the best.

"Right. So, now that that's been put aside, what do we do about you?"

No idea.

"Still set against calling on another god for help?"

Kodi hesitated before answering. The longer he spent in this brain, the more he was beginning to care about the person connected to it. He didn't know if he could just flippantly write off the fact that he'd be robbing this young man of privacy for the rest of his years, to say nothing of what prolonged exposure to the divine energies could do to him.

I don't think it would help. Nature might listen to their calls, but she might not. The only reason she'll come to me is because of the deal. Constants aren't exactly at our beck and whim.

"We could keep looking around. We know it's on the island."

We know it was on the island. Anything beyond that is pure speculation.

"Maybe I'll get another premonition?"

I doubt it; those things are unreliable even on the best day. They're like a mote of dust in the corner of your eye: the minute you begin looking for them, they disappear.

"So we're just screwed?"

Unless Fate or someone else up there intervenes, yeah, I don't see any shot of us finding that pear today.

"Clint? What are you doing here?"

Clint looked up to see Dr. Kaia Hale standing over him, a small length of cloth wrapped around her wrist. She looked disheveled to say the least: a night of drinking, a day of studying, and an afternoon of assault can take its toll on a girl. "I see Falcon over there, too. Shouldn't you all still be vacationing on Kenowai?"

Clint stared up at the woman's pleasant curved face. He had to fight back a series of insane giggles. It was just so bizarre to see someone who had existed before all this, before the gods talking to him and the cats that were kings and the wild chase for a pear. She had existed when this was all just fluff and ceremony in a world completely alien from one he currently occupied. She looked down with confusion and concern as his mouth twisted between a chuckle, a smile, and a sob.

"It's a long, impossible story," Clint said at last. "One I don't think you'd believe anyway."

"Try me." Kaia felt something, a tickle of hope in the gaping hole left behind when the pear was ripped away. She'd nearly forgotten about the rest of the legend. Maybe her only thread to something bigger hadn't been severed entirely; maybe there was still a frayed strand that could support her weight.

"Okay." Why not? At this point, one more person thinking he was off the deep end was so low on his list of concerns that Clint may as well give her the truth. "It all started after that ceremony. You see, for some reason it actually worked and Kodi was-"

"Cody?"

"Kodiwandae got too cumbersome to keep saying, so he let us use a nickname."

"The god of Kenowai told you to use a nickname?"

"Told you that you wouldn't believe me. Anyway, I wake up and he starts talking to me about finishing the ceremony and how he needs to get reunited with his realm. So after we get past the initial shock, he says he needs to go get the pear from the ceremony because it's the only way he- Ooof."

The "Ooof" in this circumstance was an exhalation of both surprise and pleasure as Dr. Kaia Hale surged forward onto Clint with a forceful kiss. It was quite proper (no tongue), but there was a ferocity in it Clint wouldn't have suspected the good doctor was concealing.

188

"I'm not crazy," Kaia muttered as she rose from the depths of the embrace. "I knew I wasn't crazy. I knew it wasn't just an electrical storm. I knew something bigger was going on."

"Uh bu wha?" Clint was not exactly the fastest man at recovering his mental faculties after such assaults. Across the room, Falcon and Mano were staring unabashedly at the curious sight. They watched with some humor as Clint shook his head to steady himself then finally located coherent words. "You knew?"

"I didn't know – not *Know* know - but I suspected, of course. It was just too strange, the way the storm popped up, the way the electronics were wrecked, and of course, the pear's strange coloration."

"You saw the pear?"

It was Kaia's turn to leap in surprise as a wholly different voice exited Clint's mouth. She was faster at acclimation than he, though, so she didn't stumble on her thoughts as this new information was assimilated.

"I did; it was glowing a strange golden color. That's why I took it from the altar in the first place."

"You've got the pear!?!" Clint leapt from his own seat and swallowed Kaia in a lung-crushing hug. "Thank you, thank you, thank you. We've chased the pear here and then we lost the trail and now we were sure we'd never get

189

it back but you have it so we can go to Denilale and I can finally go back to normal and thank you!"

Kaia laid her hand gently on Clint's narrow back. "Had."

"Beg pardon?"

"I had the pear. Past tense. Justin Goodwin stole it from me half an hour ago. That's how my wrist got sprained."

"But... how... why... how... no..." Clint's body slumped against Kaia, the power in his muscles replaced by despair. Just like that, he was no long hugging her in joy; she was now embracing him in a vain attempt at comfort.

"I don't know. Someone hired them to get it away from me. That's all I've got."

"So that's it then. That's really it. No trail, no idea where they went, only certainty that they'll be turning it over to some mystery person that we don't have any information on. It's over."

"Not quite, bro," Thunder said, tufts of hair poking through the bandages of his newly-wrapped head. April was at his side, looking profoundly more relaxed than she had when screaming at the doctors that she wasn't letting him out of her sight until she knew he was okay.

"Thunder, you okay?" Clint realized the others had gathered close during his conversation with Kaia, apparently quite interested in this new development.

"He's fine. The doctor said he's got an unnaturally thick skull that helped him absorb the blow," April answered for him.

"Gift from Pop's side," Thunder said, presumably to explain. "But dudsey, there's still a way to get back the pear."

"What?"

"Well, this whole day the wind's been blowing like a hooker trying to finance a house. Guessing that means slap-choppy seas and waves that make a surfer hard."

"So what?" Clint still wasn't getting the connection.

"So, we're on an island," Kaia said, realization dawning. "An island with only one port for local vessels. An island they might not have gotten off of yet."

"Bingo Dingo," Thunder said with a thumbs-up.

"We've still got a chance," Clint said slowly.

We do if we hurry!

"Okay then, let's go!"

"You know, some of us are here because we're feeling very ill and don't appreciate all the jumping, kissing, yelling, and antics," an old woman three chairs over from them remarked.

"Um, right. Very sorry, ma'am. We'll get out of here right away," Clint apologized.

The group vacated the hospital waiting room immediately, leaving only the old woman who had complained, a carpenter who had drilled a nail through his hand, and pair of teens who were worried they had overdosed on mushrooms. The last pair was consequently not paying much attention to what was going on in this vein of reality.

"Honestly," the old woman remarked to the carpenter. "Kids today." The carpenter nodded to keep from crying out in pain.

17.

"I don't give a damn about the weather, we'll take our chances!" Dustin yelled at the harbormaster, an older man with skin the sea had weathered and beaten without mercy. His dark eyes sparkled through the scowl on his face; despite the public nature of his job, he took a curious joy in telling land-lovers who thought they knew more than he did right where they could shove it.

The Goodwin brothers were in the harbormaster's office, a small room near the edge of the docks that was filled with filing cabinets and sun-stained yellow papers. It was hot in here; of course, it was hot everywhere in this region, but in these walls the heat seemed malicious, like it knew you had to stand here and take this small wrinkly man's bullshit and it wanted to get in its own licks as well. They'd intended to skip right past his office and set sail immediately, but the industrial-sized metal lock on a thick metal chain securing their boat to one of the piers had forced a significant change in plans.

"Look, the winds are too rough right now for me to let you leave. Even if they weren't, it wouldn't change anything." The harbormaster hoisted out a thick ledger and dropped it onto his desk with an audible "thunk." He strolled through the pages, arriving at one in the middle of the book. He flipped it around and stuck his pointed thumb on a line near the top of the page. "See? Captain Johannes docked that boat with me, and only Captain Johannes is going to get back the key to the lock placed on it." The harbormaster had taken to locking up boats that came in for safety. The thing being kept safe just happened to be the port fees that many sailors felt they were entitled to skip out on for one reason or another. Funny how after he latched their vessels to the docks revenue for the port had increased by two hundred percent.

The other brother stepped up to the table now, his face merely pinched while the other's was red in fury. Then again, it might be red in something else; they both looked like they had some nasty swelling around their eyes.

"We paid that man a handsome sum of money to bring us here and back to Kenowai," Justin said, his eyes wandering across the page's entries. "Now that we're ready to return, he has become conspicuously absent."

The harbormaster wasn't exactly surprised by this. It was a fool who paid for a return trip in advance, especially when dealing with Captain "One-More-Round-Of-Whiskey" Johannes. "So what would you have me do? Let you steal his boat because you're having trouble finding him?"

"We can leave money for it," Dustin offered. They'd barely tapped into the considerable operating budget Lawrence had provided them.

The harbormaster licked his lips, lips that had been stained forever-salty and chapped by his years serving the mighty blue seas. It was rare that one had the opportunity to

194

make the profit from selling a boat without incurring any of its initial costs. Johannes was insured, as were all the ships that lasted more than one storm season here, so two foreigners making off with his vessel could play out well for the both of them.

"I won't be letting you take advantage of him. If you want his boat, I'll make sure you pay a fair amount for it. I plan to treat it like it was my own boat I was selling to you."

Justin nodded his head understandingly. "I wouldn't have expected anything less."

*   *   *

Lawrence trekked along the rain-soaked road, the last village he'd passed fading steadily into the distance. Thankfully, the showers had ceased before he arrived, but he had an umbrella strapped to his back just in case. This region was known for unpredictable weather; some said it was retribution for a joke Felbren had played on a cloud god many centuries ago. Of course, most of the downfalls of the islands were heaped on Felbren's shoulders through one story or another. Lawrence had read through all of them that morning, poring over every detail with exceptional care, looking for a few specific pieces of information. He'd gotten what he needed, though in the process he'd also begun to suspect that Felbren was less of a trickster god than a scapegoat god. Even if he was as precocious as the legends told, the idea that he could never become savvier in his methods to avoid retribution was ridiculous.

Lawrence paused to check the map he'd copied from one of the books that morning. It looked as though he were on the right path, but who could tell with the way the rain washed and redefined the roads? Fleetingly, he wondered if he should have hired a guide, then realized how insane such an inclination was. What would he have done, taken the poor boy with him then let him watch as Lawrence met with a god? No, his only options at that point would have been... well, they would have been time-consuming to do properly, and Lawrence was running on a tight schedule. He decided he would trust his navigating skills and the old map's information to guide him forward. Lawrence was excellent at finding his way through foreign terrain, a skill he'd picked up along with many others during his time in the public sector. That had been some time ago, but he was confident the skills hadn't atrophied beyond all usefulness.

A quick adjustment of his backpack and Lawrence was plodding away once again. The grey clouds gathered overhead, threatening to soak him but never quite following through. Perhaps they got the same vibe that most people got from Lawrence, that the stretched, thin smile was the tip of an iceberg no being wanted to see the depths of. Or perhaps it was just the way the wind was blowing. Either way, Lawrence would make it most of the way to the temple before the first cloud mustered up the gumption to begin releasing its load.

*   *   *

Justin resisted the urge to whistle as he clutched the heavy grey key in his right hand. It took some serious effort though. He was feeling uncharacteristically upbeat, thanks in part to the pear sitting in the knapsack he had slung over his shoulder. The rest of his cheerful mood was due to the excitement of getting to purchase brand new state of the art equipment for their business, plus an extra bit of joy from an entry he'd happened to notice when looking at the harbor master's ledger.

"Justin, we missed the turn for our pier," Dustin called.

"We didn't miss it; we just have something else to take care of first."

"What's left to do? We got the pear, got the key, and bribed the harbormaster not to stop us when we set sail."

"Yes, but the winds are beginning to settle down, so others will likely be allowed to leave port soon as well."

"So what? You think the girl will chase us?"

"Certainly not; but it appears we aren't the only ones after this little glowing fruit," Justin replied, turning down a different dock and looking at the numbers attached to each of the massive silver locks.

"You think Lawrence hired someone else?"

"I doubt it. Though he did forewarn us that the contestants would be looking for the pear too."

"Sure, but they had no way to know it was with the good doctor, let alone that she'd jumped islands."

"I thought so." Justin stopped in front of a nice, fairly new boat. It was considerably larger than the one he and Dustin had traveled on; theirs was little more than a rowboat with an engine that left three passengers very uncomfortably cramped. "However, I feel fairly certain that it was not someone else with the name 'Thunder' that signed this boat into the harbormaster's log."

"That's my brother, always catching the minute details." Dustin stepped forward to admire the sea-vessel in a new light. "Should we steal it?"

"If only we could. Somehow a man who lashes boats to piers when their owners are away strikes me as a bit too smart to use locks that take the same key." Justin tried his key on the lock anyway, just to make sure. His suspicions were confirmed when it wouldn't even fit all the way inside, let alone turn.

"Too bad, it looks a lot more comfortable than ours."

"Agreed. Still, just because we can't make use of it doesn't mean we have to let it become a tool against us."

"You know, Justin, I think I saw a few small anchors laying on the deck of a boat a few yards back."

"Did you, now? I think we might just have some use for them." People often thought Dustin was stupid, and while Justin agreed that his brother was dumber and quicker to anger than he, it didn't mean Dustin didn't have the occasional spark of insight. Justin felt a twinge of pride as Dustin hustled down the dock and leapt aboard the unattended small ship. He returned seconds later dragging a pair of anchors roughly the width of extra-large tennis racket. Justin accepted one then tested the heft of it in his hand. Yes indeed, this would do an excellent job.

"You first," Dustin offered.

"No, I think you deserve the first swing," Justin countered. "You're the reason we succeeded, after all. If you hadn't held off that crowd, I doubt I ever would have tracked her down in time."

Dustin beamed with pride so brightly that for a moment the birds floating around them thought a new lighthouse had been installed. He walked onto the boat with a look of determination and raised the anchor high over his head, eyes unwaveringly locked on the wooden floor beneath his feet. Justin looked on with pride as his brother demolished someone else's property.

In different circumstances it might have been quite a touching moment.

*   *   *

Lawrence was at the temple's gates when his phone rang. He was impressed he still got reception this far out, but then again, he hadn't sprung for the ultra-mobile model for nothing. Lawrence knew quite well that an operation could be made or destroyed based on how effective its communication was.

He paused in front of the moderately-sized stone building, an ornate opening before him that seemed to descend further back into the mountain it jutted out from. For all the talk of Felbren as an annoyance, the people of his island still clearly had enough faith that he looked over them to go to some impressive lengths. That, or this had been constructed for some earlier, greater god and Felbren's followers had merely moved in over time. Both seemed reasonably viable.

He pulled out the phone to see Justin Goodwin's number glowing in blue letters across the screen. About time; he'd expected this call hours ago. Lawrence clicked the "accept" button with his thumb.

"Yes?" He paused, listening to Justin's cocky voice over the background of waves slapping against wood. "Excellent. Where are you?" Lawrence adjusted his supplies so they weren't cutting into his shoulder. "I see. Well, you know where to go next. What about the girl?" He doubted Kaia was any threat; to be honest, Lawrence wasn't certain she'd even known what she had. "You can? The others too? Be careful not to be followed." Justin's voice was doing everything but giving itself a hand job with all the ego flowing through it. "I see. Well, aren't you thorough? Just be certain that-"

This time Justin's voice was filled with shock as he yelped into the microphone. Lawrence pulled the phone from his ear and cursed. He waited until Justin seemed to have calmed down then resumed his conversation. "What happened? Slow down, what did the beer do?"

There was another sound from Justin, this one not a screech or a yelp but a moan. Lawrence knew that moan; he'd inspired more of them than he would generally admit to. It was the guttural wrenching of someone who had just realized the precariousness of their situation and the fragility of life. Lawrence closed his phone and slid it back into his pocket. Any more conversation was a waste of time; he had learned everything he needed to simply from that moan.

Lawrence headed forward into the maw of the mountain, the open temple door engulfing him in stale darkness after only a few steps.

*   *   *

"Mother fuckers!" Thunder yelled, shaking his first angrily at the white shape bobbing on the sea and the two men grinning gleefully within it.

His sentiment well summed up the feelings of the group. They'd barely missed the brothers, arriving just as they were pulling away from the dock. Thunder had been ready to leap in after them, but April had pointed out his injury and Mano had reminded him that swimming on rough water in the middle of piers with wooden beams everywhere was just asking for trouble. Instead, they'd run to get their own boat, only to find floating splinters where it had been docked. The largest chunk was a piece of the bow that was still chained in place; the rest had been claimed by Iohalo.

"I dug that boat!" Thunder shouted.

"Damn it," Kaia swore. "If only we'd been faster."

"We ran as hard as we could," Clint pointed out. "I'm not sure what more we could have done."

"Is it me or are they lifting something at us?" April squinted and leaned forward slightly, neither actually improving her vision but still making her feel as though they had.

"They seem to be toasting us with beer cans," Falcon said. Her own eyesight was excellent despite the advance of years her eyes had endured. One might wonder if it was part of why she'd chosen the name Falcon to begin with; however, it was probably just a coincidence. "Actually, it looks like the same beer the fisherman gave us with the boat."

"They stole our beer? That is just dropping insult on injury!" Thunder doubled the enthusiasm of his fist shaking.

Amidst their ranting and curses, Mano stood silent, staring out at the water. When they'd first seen the boat, he'd imagined he saw something, a fleeting shape among the waves. His eyes kept scanning the water carefully, searching for confirmation of his suspicions. He was probably wrong; this was the wrong part of the sea and way too close to the docks. The odds against it were staggering. Still... Mano had seen firsthand that odds didn't matter so much when you were the one in a million. Besides, after everything he'd done in the last day with this group of wackjobs, maybe it was time he took his own leap of faith.

"Hey, Clint, I've got a question."

"What's up, Mano?"

203

"That voice thing: how far is the range?"

"No idea." There was a brief pause, and then the other voice came from Clint's mouth.

"The farther away something is, the weaker the effect will be. If you're thinking of sinking the ship, forget it. The most I could do is turn it over, but it's small enough that they could flip it right back and barely be annoyed."

"I think I have another idea. Fair warning, it's probably crazy."

Clint laughed, a genuine bark of humor that was snatched up by the wind and carried down the coast to cheer whatever lucky ears heard it. "At this point, I don't think I would trust a non-crazy idea anyway. Lay it on us."

*   *   *

"Look at those dipshits on the dock. I wish I could see their faces better." Dustin didn't half-ass his gloating, going full on with the enjoyment of seeing the others' frustrations.

"Be quiet, I'm calling Lawrence," Justin said, one hand cupping the phone to his face and the other burying a finger in his free ear. The damned ocean might be pretty and a convenient means of escape, but it made it hard to hear. At last the electronic ringing in his ear gave way to a click and a voice. "Lawrence, it's Justin. We've got the pear."

"Hell yeah we did," Dustin said, pulling out some beers from the case they'd liberated from the other boat before sending it all to the ocean's floor.

"We're on a boat off the coat of Alendola." Justin's eyes flickered back to the shoreline where the mini-mob was still stymied in frustration. "She's no issue. We sank their boat; in fact, I can see her and the others stuck on the dock right now." They appeared to have stopped yelling, Justin noticed, and were clustering around Clint and the island boy. He wasn't sure why, but he didn't like that.

All at once there was a… a something that rippled out from the shore. It wasn't anything that could be seen or heard; it was more like Justin felt his stomach drop out for a moment, as though he were on a roller coaster for less than a half of a heartbeat. He shook it off easily, chalking it up to the boat's insufferable rocking, and tried to focus on what Lawrence was saying. This effort was cut short by another interruption, this one far less ethereal.

Justin and Dustin both let out yelps as the beer they'd stolen exploded from the cans, showering all over the boat, their bodies, and the open sea. Every can detonated simultaneously, leading Justin to briefly wonder if the others had somehow foreseen these events and stuffed tiny explosives in the alcohol. Then he realized just how insane that theory was and got back to business.

"Sorry about that," Justin said hurriedly. "The beer blew up for some reason, it caught us off guard."

Lawrence was saying something else, but Justin was distracted by his brother, who was frantically signaling for his attention. Justin was about to tell his brother to shut up when he felt something bump their boat. He glanced into the water and let out a low, miserable groan. Somewhere in the back of his brain he registered the click from the other end of the line as Lawrence hung up on him; however, that tidbit of trivia was being filed away for consideration at a much later date, if there was one. Justin wasn't counting on any future activities as the hammerhead shark circling their suddenly too-small and too-frail boat slammed against it once more, sending Justin and Dustin tumbling to the wooden base.

Both brothers clutched at the small seats, gaining a considerable number of splinters for their efforts. Justin's phone began ringing again; he glanced down and was surprised to see "Dr. Kaia Hale" appear on the screen. He'd forgotten that less than two days ago they'd been coworkers, here to do something as innocuous as shoot a commercial. Of course he had her number, but why was she calling right now? To gloat? No, that's what he or Dustin would do; she was more decent. She could clearly see the danger they were in; maybe as a local she knew some trick to make the shark lose interest.

Justin snatched the phone up right before the next bump, this one violently tipping them to one side before they mercifully settled back in the right-side up position. "Help us!" Justin yelled into the phone, all sense of composure and cunning savaged away by the shark situation.

Kaia's voice, in contrast, was smooth and confident as she spoke to her former attacker. "Mano says if you turn around right now and come back to the dock, you might get back before his friend tips you over."

"His friend?" Justin was about to protest the lunacy of such a statement, but another hard knock forced him to realign his priorities. "Okay, fine, you win, we'll turn back. I'm just not sure that we'll make it."

"Mano says if you toss the remaining beer cans and what is in them out into the water, one by one as you go, then you might just get here."

"You're insane. All of you are completely off-the-wall, batshit insane."

"Fucking right." The cold slush of New York that had infected Kaia was beginning to slip through her voice. "And Justin? If you look, even for a second, like you're thinking about going anywhere other than the pier right in front us, Mano will have his friend devour you two and shit you out as krill food."

"What about the pear?" Justin had one trump card left and he would be damned if he didn't play it.

"Sharks don't eat fruit. Start rowing, asshole."

* * *

Handling the Goodwins proved to be a rather simple matter once they reached the dock. It seemed the experience of being pursued by a shark like little more than mobile appetizers took a significant bit of the fight out of them. Mano and Thunder relieved Justin of his backpack as soon they were on the wooden dock, Mano pausing only long enough to pour the remaining beer into the water. The dark shape trailing beneath the waves slipped over to them, enjoying the remaining liquid as it dispersed in the water.

"When I get back to Kenowai I am going to dump a whole case in the ocean for you," Mano promised his finned friend.

"I'll kick in one as well," Kaia said. Her wrist seemed to hurt a bit less as she watched the brothers scramble across the wooden slats, desperate to get to dry land and safety from the razor-toothed menace. They made it about ten steps before the others circled around them.

"You tried to steal the pear," April accused. "We're not letting you get away with that."

"It's just a pear, that's barely a crime," Justin sniped back.

"Assaulting our friend is a big one, though," Clint pointed out.

"Plus, you deep dropped our boat," Thunder added.

"You don't have proof of either of those things," Dustin said.

"Actually, we do," Kaia said, her hand rummaging through the backpack Mano had handed off to her. At last her fingers closed around a well-known shape that emitted a familiar current. It was strange to think she'd once been unsure if that energy was really there; the minute she touched the pear this time she could feel it flowing all the way down to her bones. "In case you forgot, I'm the one you beat up, and trust me when I say the local authorities will be more inclined to believe me than you."

Dustin opened his mouth to protest, but Justin cut him off with a quick motion. "Fine; you can get us arrested, possibly even prosecuted. Since you didn't call the cops while we were rowing in, I trust you want something else from us instead."

"We want to know why you stole the pear. Who hired you, how'd they know, the whole nine yards," Clint demanded.

Justin sneered. "You want us to give you all that just to beat a trumped-up misdemeanor assault charge? Thanks, but no thanks. Go ahead and call the cops."

Clint looked at the others and shrugged. "Well, we tried to do it the nice way." He started walking forward. Justin and Dustin braced themselves to resist, and immediately found Mano and Thunder at their sides.

"No go, bro."

"It would be best if you relaxed for this and did not struggle," Mano encouraged.

"What the hell are you talking about?" Dustin was looking a bit uncertain. For the first time in a long time, his brother didn't seem to be in control of their situation.

Clint stopped directly in front of Justin, then reached down and took his hand. Justin felt a strange pulse run across his skin as Clint's eyes closed and concentration spread across his face.

"Now then, let's see what secrets you've been hiding."

*　　　*　　　*

Felbren didn't appear in a flash of lighting or a swirl of energy; instead he merely stepped out of the corner of the temple, like he'd been hunched over waiting for someone to call and had heard his cue. His 'cue', in this case, was a small cup of whiskey, a slice of fine meat, and an apple left on his altar, all of which had been incanted over. Lawrence preferred to think of them as incantations rather than prayers because praying implied a certain level of faith, and at this point he was working from knowledge rather than Belief.

The medium-statured god looked the same as he had in the dream; even his clothes were identical. Immortal beings, much like geniuses, have better things to occupy themselves with than fashion. Most simply find a look that suits them and stick with it.

"*You're here early.*" Felbren helped himself to the offering, starting with the meat which sizzled in his hands then washing it down with the whiskey.

"I came to tell you that my people failed and Kodiwandae has the pear."

Felbren cocked an eyebrow. "*You traveled to my island to tell me that? Most people try to avoid giving a god bad news in person. It doesn't really play out too well.*"

Lawrence took a seat on one of the stone benches that littered the area. Other men might have seen a threat in Felbren's words; Lawrence only saw opportunity. "It was a difficult prospect from the beginning. All I had was some petty cash and a few young men with able bodies and useless minds. That against a crew of people with the knowledge of a god is something of a tall order."

"Kodiwandae is a soft-hearted fool; he should have posed no threat without his power."

"So it's your contention that the wisdom of a god is something that mortals can easily overcome?"

Felbren bristled a little at this remark. *"Certainly not. That is why someone of your caliber was contracted."*

"With all due respect, gods are the ones that make miracles. I specialize in finding solutions. Given the challenges present, I found the option most likely to succeed. In this case, even the best turned out to be not that likely."

"I see. Well, excuses or not, you've failed me, Fixer." Felbren took one last swallow of the whiskey and knocked the apple from the altar; he didn't really care for fruit. The god began to consider what the best way to turn this human into an example would be.

"Actually, I haven't failed you yet. The job isn't over until Kodiwandae regains his power. That means they have to get to Denilale. That's why I'm here; I thought of a solution that has a much better chance of stopping them."

"Make sure it's a good one, mortal; this will be your last chance."

Instead of speaking, Lawrence reached into his bag and produced a clear canteen filled with sea water and a large pink pearl. He set both down on the bench beside him then looked at Felbren, whose face was growing steadily angrier.

"You dare come into my temple and attempt to capture me?"

"Capture? Never would such an idea occur to me," Lawrence said quickly. "I was reading up on you, though. Funny thing about trickster gods: there's a lot more information on how to dispel or stop them than there is about other gods. I read the story of how you broke a thousand pearls looking for a pink one to give to Alahai, how Iohalo cursed you in retribution so that if you ever drank sea water with a pink pearl in it, you would be sealed in the pearl for three full moons or until the pearl was broken. They even said a human who held that pearl would be able to use a trifle of your power."

"Bringing up old wounds is not a way to lessen my wrath."

"You want to stop Kodiwandae? This is the key. I've found a few stories where this weakness was used on you, and in many of them your captors would hop between the islands after it was over, going home and showing off the pearl or on to another adventure."

"*So?*"

"So it seems Iohalo's banishment from the ocean doesn't apply when you are sealed in the pearl. It occurred to me the best way to contend with a god is with a stronger god."

Felbren's temper receded slightly; the mortal made a good point. He could always teleport back to his island, but leaving it was a rare opportunity. Those damnable punks who'd shanghaied him into the pearl before had indeed moved him across the waves without incurring the sea god's wrath. There was still a large logistical problem to surmount, however.

"*Suppose I did let you carry me to Denilale. A man such as yourself might be tempted to keep me sealed so as to use the small bit of my power for himself.*"

"That's where you're wrong. While I won't deny the prospect would be tempting for anyone, myself included, it takes a man like myself to rise above any temptations and keep the bigger goal in mind. If I screw you over, I get a few months of parlor tricks until the curse is released. If I uphold my end of the bargain, I get back my youth and a small mountain of gold, as we agreed."

"Even a small bit of my power amounts to considerably more than parlor tricks," Felbren corrected.

"Forgive me; I just meant it doesn't compare to what I'd get from completing our deal."

"You are a powerfully rational man."

"I look at the risk and gain in a situation and determine the best course of action. In this case, you risk a few months of imprisonment, but you gain the chance to slow Kodiwandae's ascension. I risk getting hurt or killed in the process, but I gain the chance at shedding some years off this tired old body."

Felbren walked over to the bench and picked up the canteen, removing the cap with a simple twist. He took a small swig of the water, the salty contents telling him it indeed came from the ocean. He plucked the pink pearl from the bench and stared at the elderly mortal before him.

"If they have the pear, we'll have to hurry. My island is the farthest from Denilale."

"I've already got a fast boat waiting for us. We'll beat them there by half a day at least."

Felbren nodded and dropped the pearl into the canteen. He regarded it one last time then gave a shrug. The human was right; even if he betrayed Felbren, it would at most cost him a few months. What was that compared to a chance at Alahai's heart? Felbren took a long, deep draw of the water, his body immediately growing less solid as his essence began to flow toward the pearl.

For Lawrence it was like what he always imagined something going into a black hole would look like. Felbren began flowing through the top of the canteen, his form extending like smoke then swirling about the pearl. As fast as it flowed, the pearl took it in at equal measure, the pink sphere giving off a gentle glow as it funneled an entire god into its depths. The whole process was over in fewer than five seconds, leaving the canteen to drop to the ground as the hand holding it was sucked away.

Lawrence carefully picked up the container then poured its contents across his hand. The pearl dropped into his wrinkled fingers and his hand closed around it. He felt gentle warmth coming from the object, one that suffused his whole body. Yes, it was easy to see why Felbren had been worried Lawrence would be tempted to keep him bound so as not to lose this feeling. That wasn't going to happen, however; Lawrence always kept his eyes on the end-game.

It took him a few minutes to re-pack his items and leave the temple. In the time he'd been inside the rain had finally begun to pour in earnest. Lawrence reached from his umbrella then stayed his hand. Instead he clutched the pearl and willed a rain-proof dome into existence over his head. He took a tentative step outside and found the drops crashing against some invisible force before they could make contact with him. Lawrence smiled his terrifying smile: this he could get used to. He wouldn't do it by simply keeping Felbren trapped in a pearl, though; that would be silly. Of course, he wasn't going to settle for just his youth back, either; that would be naïve.

No, Lawrence had his own plan, one that was going swimmingly so far. Lawrence had devoured the myths of this island and believed he'd found quite the useful opportunity buried among the texts. A god would be ascending in Denilale tomorrow, all right, but it wouldn't be Kodiwandae. That lovesick fool had squandered his opportunity. It was time for a new god to rise: one with vision, one with ambition, one who knew how to get things done. It was time for a god like Lawrence Farran.

*   *   *

"Still no ideas on why Lawrence would want the pear?"

Not a one. It's only a scrap of my power, so it's not as though he could eat it and gain more than a temporary smattering of magic. He'd need the ability to wield divine energy to actually use it to call Nature, and even then, without me present, whose favor would he be trying to gain? My best guess is that he merely doesn't realize what it can and can't do, so he's chasing it in ignorance.

Clint suppressed a shudder as he remembered the older man's calm, confident eyes. "He doesn't strike me as the type to do things without proper research."

When faced with the fantastical, many people have been known to make erroneous assumptions.

"I guess so." Clint could have debated the point further; however, it wouldn't have yielded anything useful. The group had bickered back and forth about Lawrence's potential reasoning after Kodi had stolen the truth from Justin's mind. No one had landed on a single concrete theory, though Thunder had been adamant it was "Bad news, dudes." They had the pear, at least, and it was hard to feel too concerned about anything else that may come their way in the afterglow of that particular triumph.

"So, how does it feel?" Clint sat on the dock, watching the sun begin to sink toward the horizon, a second light source in the form of a golden pear held firmly in his hand. The others were looking into obtaining a ride over to Denilale, but Clint had wanted a few minutes of rest. Using the voice had left his throat even sorer than the first time and he'd been left with a sense of vertigo for nearly five minutes afterward. Strangely, he'd begun to feel better almost as soon as Kaia had handed him Kodi's pear.

Good. Familiar. Like I've filled in a piece of me I didn't notice was empty.

"Sounds nice." Clint turned the fruit over in his hands, amused at the gentle tingle that emanated wherever its skin pressed against his. "If you feel like that just from the pear, how do you think you'll feel when you finally get your full power back?"

Big, expanded, powerful. It's like going from being a rock drifting along in the river to being one of the currents. You become connected to a flow you can only suspect existed beforehand.

"Speaking as one of the rocks, I do have to say that sounds enjoyable."

It is. It really is. Still, this experience has been enlightening.

Clint looked out at the steadily darkening ocean, where somewhere in its depths was a hammerhead shark with an impressive passion for beer. "It has been interesting."

Very interesting. It's also been fascinating to see life from the mortal point of view. For how little time you all get here, most of you pack quite a bit of living into it.

"Most of us?"

I'm not really telling you anything you don't know when I say that this isn't just the biggest adventure in your adult life, it's your only one.

"And it's pretty much over. All that's left is to get to the temple and make the call."

Barring any more involvement from Lawrence, it should be smooth sailing from here.

"Isn't it considered bad luck to say that sort of thing? Like you're challenging fate."

Well, for one thing, I didn't say it loud so I doubt it counts. Even if it does, I'm pretty sure such things don't apply to gods.

"Let's hope so." Clint rose slowly from the dock and began heading toward the harbor master's office where the others were negotiating enthusiastically. "I've got to get back home pretty soon."

Yes, I saw your friend's predicament when I was looking through your memories. I'm sorry for her illness.

"It's okay. No one lives forever… well, none of us humans, at any rate." Another person, most other people, would have had some bitterness in their tone at that remark. Clint did not. He didn't feel jealousy or anger toward Kodiwandae for having something he never would. That would have required desire, and even now Clint smelled greasepaint and blood when he danced too close to that line.

Gods fall too. Endings and beginning are inevitable for all beings, save only for the Constants.

"Then I suppose the most we can do is make sure tomorrow is a spectacular beginning."

I've heard worse ideas.

Clint put the pear in the backpack slung across his shoulders, the one that had formerly belonged to Justin before he and his brother had run screaming from the dock after Kodi's mind probe. Clint didn't want to explain the curious color of the fruit to any passers-by; he had a feeling his next day would already be full enough as it was.

18.

While Kenowai was a rural community with lush surroundings, Alendola was a more modern civilization that still prized its beaches. As the charter boat deposited Clint and his friends on Denilale, however, it became apparent that this island was composed of a few determined villages desperately pushing back a jungle. The vegetation seeped into the town, even near the port, purposely blurring the lines between where mankind ruled and where it had to tread softly. The port city was actually quite sprawling and cosmopolitan; however, the plethora of vines and bushes cluttering the roads made it feel disjointed, like several small villages might have happened to crop up right next to one another. The buildings were all stone: not the colorful mosaics of Alendola, but hand-carved granite that had been chosen for its durability rather than its aesthetic. These were homes and business that could weather everything from a monsoon to a tiger attack, and the scars lashed across the surfaces said quite plainly that many had done just that.

It was also notable that while Kenowai had the occasional upward slope that manifested in a hill, and Alendola was renowned for its gently rolling terrain, only Denilale could boast of its mountainous heights. It was at the peak of one such earthen spike that a large temple dedicated to the goddess of the land was kept by its people. In most cases these shrines were used to pray for ample growth among the land's plants: this one was dedicated to asking for the vegetation to stay in check. The people had abundant fruits and vegetable provided by the ground; what they didn't have were many areas where they could take their children for a walk without stepping into a lush green world that could easily turn into a deathtrap.

Finding a guide proved to be no real challenge; the locals were accustomed to tourists making trips over to their island in hopes of a greater spiritual experience. In a matter of hours, they'd gotten supplies and trekked most of the way up the carved path in the mountain's face. There were occasional moments where the guides would stop them, listening to some noise unheard by those not accustomed to living lower on the food chain, then usher them forward rapidly.

Everyone was tense as they made their way; it seemed like after all that had happened it was unavoidable that some last hurdle would erupt in their path. So it was that as the temple came into view, many of them felt a mix of relief and mild disappointment flood through their systems.

We made it.

"We finally made it," Clint said, staring at the impressive building. It was made of the same material as the other buildings, but this one had ornate carvings on its side, showing that it was for more than just function. This was a place of worship as well as a defendable outpost on high ground.

"This thing is legit," Thunder complimented. He'd recovered nicely from his head injury, assuring the others he'd taken far worse blows to the head throughout the course of his life. This led to a lot of awkward coughing and staring at the ground as people tried to resist making an easy joke at the expense of the recently wounded.

"It is rather impressive," April concurred.

"I did a study on the architectural practices of Denilalians that was inspired by seeing this temple," Kaia said. "I wanted to know how they'd managed to craft something like this in such a remote location."

"How'd they do it?" Falcon asked. "Some method for moving the stones up the hill using rolling logs?"

"Nope, turns out they did it the old fashioned way: a lot of time and a lot of blood."

"Never underestimate the strength of the dedicated faithful," Mano said. He'd been rather quiet since the day before. The others understood the reason without asking. He'd seen something beyond mortal comprehension when Clint and Kodi made the beer explode. He might have believed in his gods beforehand, but the absolute evidence that something greater than himself existed had caused a bit of internal reassessment. The only thing he'd actively done on the way over was buy another case of beer and pour it in the ocean as they sailed to Denilale. Thunder and, surprisingly enough, April had lent him a hand in the endeavor. No one ever saw the dark shape they knew was trailing beneath the waves, but they made sure to keep the beer flowing all the same.

"We should hurry, there is still ground to cover," one of the three guides piped up. Kaia and Mano were able to pronounce their names, but the others had been lost after the first round of vowels. Fortunately, they'd been all business and hadn't tried for small talk, which had kept the name confusion to a minimum. The group began plodding forward once more, the temple growing steadily larger in their view as they drew closer.

Clint felt a flurry of excitement swirl through him, one he was pretty sure belonged more to Kodi than him. The line between them seemed to be getting fuzzier by the day. Clint was ready to have his body back to being a single-occupancy vehicle, but he suspected he might miss the god's more varied emotional palette. Plus, it was sort of nice always having someone to talk to. He imagined when this would be over: collecting his money and going back to Golden Acres, sitting in another office taking the blame for some business man who had royally screwed up or been screwed over.

"Maybe I should job hunt," Clint mumbled under his breath.

Why? I think your profession is quite noble.

Clint snorted. "You think being a scapegoat for hire is noble?"

From what I saw looking through your memories, it seems like you give people second chances. That is always noble.

Clint mulled the different perspective over a bit. "I never looked at it that way."

I'm sure the people you've saved have. They made mistakes, some honest, some probably less honest, but either way you give them an opportunity to do it over. That's what you're giving me, and I am very thankful for it.

"It's no big deal."

It actually is, and the sooner you see that, the happier you'll be with the path you've chosen.

"I don't think I'm-" Clint was interrupted by Thunder's lanky arm curling around his shoulders.

"Bro, the locals aren't newsed up on the current sitch. Might want to muffle the solo chatter." Thunder's voice was low and his tone friendly, but Clint took his point. They weren't finished yet, and they were being led toward a holy site. People could be a bit touchy about whom they let into such places and someone out of his mind may not make the cut.

"Sorry," Clint whispered back.

"Don't be sorry, be wowzered." Thunder pointed ahead of them and Clint realized that during his little debate they'd nearly made it to the front doors of the temple. They rose ten feet high, intricate etchings woven across the thick wooden front. The rest of the temple was engraved too, scenes of a beautiful woman surrounded by foliage commanding animals and creating harvests for her worshippers. The doors began to part as the group drew closer, revealing a large entrance hall lit by rows of torches lining the walls. The people of Denilale might have been dedicated enough to haul the materials and decorate appropriately, but there was no way they were compromising a potential stronghold with windows just for the ambiance of sunlight. In this case, however, the thick stone walls offered none of the visitors any comfort, as they recognized a familiar figure waiting for them just inside the doors.

"Good morning," Lawrence said, smiling at them casually.

Clint, Thunder, and Mano tried to rush forward as soon as they saw him; however, they discovered their bodies were no longer answering any orders. The whole group stood frozen as their guides produced bundles of rope from their satchels and set about binding their hands and feet.

What are you doing? Why are you letting him capture you?

Clint struggled to flap his tongue, but he couldn't get as much as a tremor out of it. Instead, he tried to focus on the idea of being trapped, forming images of cages and bear traps in his mind as clearly as he could. It took some effort to block out everything else, but unsurprisingly, being stuck stock still gave him a bit of extra focus.

Why won't you... ohhh, shit, you can't move, can you?

Clint waited for Kodi to realize the futility of the question.

Right, you can't answer if you are. Why wouldn't you be able to move, though? Nature doesn't have any reason to block me.

"I went ahead and warned the natives of your intentions to defile their temple," Lawrence said, stepping out and checking the knots encircling their limbs. "They were happy to assist the man their goddess had sent to stop you."

Bullshit; Nature doesn't fuck around with messengers. If she wants to make a point, she does it with dozens of sharp-toothed animals tearing a swath of carnage.

Clint might have agreed; however, the supernatural way he'd been bound seemed empirical evidence to the contrary.

"In a few moments the goddess will permit you to move your legs once more. I suggest you come along peacefully and do as you're told. We have a cleansing ceremony to perform to purge the negative energy you brought to this hallowed ground."

Go along with it for now. We'll think of something inside.

There didn't seem to be much choice anyway, so as Clint felt a tingle in his legs, he took a tentative step forward. His lower body responded, and he walked toward the great entrance hall, a hall which was no longer nearly as inviting as it had been mere moments earlier.

*   *   *

Clint didn't know where the others were: he'd been led to a separate room. The walls were stone, of course, while the ground was comprised of little more than a few dirt pits. He'd been carefully helped into one of them, though he found the further he got from Lawrence, the more mobility he had in the rest of his body. The pits weren't terribly deep: the top of one was only about a foot or so above Clint's head. It still would have been nearly impossible to safely enter alone, so Clint was actually a bit grateful for the helping hands that lowered him down to the dirt at the pit's bottom. Kodi, on the other hand, was less enthused.

I'll curse all of you into snails! I'll send plagues to your families! I'll render you all eunuchs! Get us out of here this instant!

His ranting served to do little more than give Clint a minor headache, but it seemed to make Kodi feel a little better. As soon as Clint was secured, the locals left him, walking out the doorless entryway without any conversation within their ranks. It seemed strange to Clint that they were going along with this so completely. He felt like capturing people just on the word of someone who claimed to speak for their god would have inspired at least a bit more curiosity. He wondered if whatever was restricting his movement could be suspending their disbelief as well.

I guess they're gone for now. Can you talk yet?

Clint tried his tongue and found it still sluggish and unresponsive. He could move his head a little though, so he shook it to signal a negative.

No luck, huh? Well, at least we can do yes or no this way. I guess that's improvement. I'm still trying to figure out how he's bound us like this.

Clint felt a pulse of frustration at this binding. How dare this pathetic mortal visit his will upon a higher being! Clint shook his head to wipe away Kodi's feelings. They were spilling over more fiercely as they escalated. He had to keep reminding himself that these swells of emotions weren't his own. Then again, this one might actually be happening within both of them: Clint wasn't exactly happy about being captured and stuck in a damn pit while Lawrence did who-knew-what to his friends.

He didn't have to wonder for long. Clint heard the soft step of fine leather shoes against the temple's floor coming from the room's entrance. Within a few moments, Lawrence's head poked into view from the edge of the pit.

"Comfortable? I don't want to be an ungracious host."

Clint stared up at him blankly.

"Oh, right, I suppose I should loosen things up a bit if I want to have a conversation."

Clint felt a familiar tingle across his whole body, a body he quickly discovered was once more listening to his instructions.

"Why are you doing this?"

"Pathetic mortal, you will beg for my mercy!"

Lawrence tilted his head slightly, more intrigued than surprised at the dual voices Clint was spouting. He studied the young man, noting that he seemed far more engaged than he had the last time Lawrence saw him. At dinner that night Clint had been a man on the cusp of the world, closer to living through it than living in it. This version of Clint was different: there was a bit of fire in his eyes. Whatever he'd been through in the past few days had certainly had an effect on him.

"Kodiwandae, I assume. It is a pleasure to meet you; I do hope you'll abide the momentary inconvenience."

"I will abide no such thing. Release my vessel at once and perhaps I will show some restraint in determining your punishment."

"I do hate to be rude, but I should point out that you won't be punishing anyone until after you've risen. That's a feat that you won't be accomplishing without the pear I've got stored in the other room."

"You know about that?" Clint spoke before Kodi could, hoping to steer the conversation in a direction more informative than the bickering.

"Of course; that's why I sent the Goodwins after you."

"But how? And why?"

"Sorry, my boy, I've been around a bit too long to give monologues explaining my plan. I do promise to tell it all to you afterward, though. If things go well, you shouldn't have to wait very long. All I need to know from you is one thing: what is the goddess's name?"

"What do you mean; don't they have one for her here?"

"Dalania, a name which I've already tried calling and haven't gotten any response. I suspect there's a different term she's waiting for, one that Kodiwandae, and possibly his human vessel, is aware of."

Tell him no, Clint. Tell him I never told you what it was. I'm not sure how he's pulling any of this crap, but I have an idea of what he'll do next.

"Sorry; he hasn't exactly been sharing the secrets of the universe with me."

"Pity, but no matter. The offer to surrender the information verbally was simply formality. I have other ways to get what I need." Lawrence floated up from the ground and glided into the pit, settling down only a few inches away from Clint. Clint tried to say something sarcastic; however, he discovered his body was once again not accepting orders.

"I've found along with the more impressive abilities I recently acquired, there are also a few with less flash and more usefulness. For example, I can dig through someone's memories with nothing more than a touch."

Bingo.

"I'm sure having a god in your brain could make this problematic, so before we begin, I'd like you to know that the rest of your friends are in the main room of the temple. I have no need to cause them harm - I'm not a petty man after all. If your divine friend should try anything that renders me unable to return in the next five minutes, however, they'll be killed one at a time. Something to bear in mind."

If Clint could have gulped, he would have. He really hoped Kodi wasn't going to do anything stupid.

I heard him. Don't worry about it; have a little faith in me.

As Lawrence's hand settled on Clint's face, he tried very hard to muster up some semblance of faith. He wasn't trying to believe in Kodiwandae, he was just trying to believe in a general fairness of the world, that something in the universal system of existence would stop this man from getting his way. Clint tried with all his heart to Believe, but all he felt inside was scared. Scared for his friends, scared for Kodiwandae, and scared for the world that was facing a man like Lawrence with powers like these.

"Let's begin."

*   *   *

Thunder's life-changing moment hadn't come in the form of watching a clown get into a brawl or a near-death experience with a shark. In fact, to anyone watching from the outside, his moment would have seemed completely mundane. Such is the problem with seeing only what rests on the surface.

Though his body was twenty-three years old, Thunder had only existed for five of them. Before his moment, he had been someone else entirely. Not-Thunder was a quiet young man, studious, organized, and dedicated to his work. He made his father constantly proud with his wit and academic prowess, securing a spot in a prestigious university without even having to resort to using the family connections. He was on track for a successful corporate life. He was a child any parent would be happy to show off. He was perfect.

He was miserable. Work, books, papers, rinse, repeat. Life was like tofu: nutritious, but lacking flavor. Not-Thunder was smart enough to be self-aware; he knew he wasn't happy. What he couldn't figure out was why. He came from wealth, there was a bright future ahead of him, he was in good health. There was no objective reason he could discern why he shouldn't be happy. It wasn't until college that Not-Thunder had the idea that would change everything.

With a sampling of like-aged students as big as his university offered, he could conduct a study: catalogue people from various walks of life, plot their respective contentment, find the common denominator in those with the highest scores, and incorporate it into his own life. This was the kind of idea that most people would have laughed off, but Not-Thunder was far from most people. He was an achiever, and this was something he wanted to achieve.

It took months of work to get all the data he needed. Interviews, surveys, analysis of a myriad of nearly untrackable factors, all had to be balanced with maintaining his grades. It was a darn good thing Not-Thunder was smart, otherwise he would have failed out. Still, he kept at it, and by March he had finally generated a defendable output from his study.

That was his moment: sitting in the library amidst people talking about their plans for spring break, checking and re-checking his data. To anyone observing, he seemed to be focusing on a particularly important assignment. They wouldn't be wrong in that evaluation, not technically; they would just never truly grasp the depth of how important it was.

For his part, Not-Thunder could scarcely believe what his work told him. The happiest people he'd measured were the ones who never seemed to think about their happiness. The ones who lived in action, who made choices that were often the very epitome of stupidity. Especially worth noting was a nearly-universally high rating amidst those who participated in the fraternity and sorority lifestyles. Though some of them were quite intelligent, it was that single factor that seemed to most determine how content they were with life: the willingness to act. Taking chances, even when they rarely paid off, still generated more joy than careful analysis and preparation.

Applying the theorem to his own life, Not-Thunder realized the pattern held true. All he did was plan and prepare for the life he would one day have. He was treating his youth like it was the night before an important presentation, building a strong base of knowledge for when all eyes eventually turned to him. But… would that ever happen? His father managed his company from an upper suite that didn't permit most other employees to interact with him. The man went to socials with other wealthy people who were keeping others at arm's length. There was no warmth, no impulse, no life. And that was where Not-Thunder was heading. He was preparing for life, but on this path he was never going to live it. The data was right there in front of him. Data didn't lie.

The next Fall there was a new face at one of the less academically rigorous colleges in Dallas. He wore a bright pink collared shirt, silver aviators, and flip-flops with beer openers in the bottom. This young man was noted among the frat he rushed as the most enthusiastic of all the pledges in his class; really, the most gung-ho participant that any of them could remember. No matter what trial the brothers organized, he was jumping up and down to participate. It wasn't that he had no shame or lacked common sense: he was just sincerely happy to be there. Sure, he had a strange way of speaking, and his name was ridiculous, but the guy bubbled with happiness. It made everyone else a little more cheerful just having him around. Thunder was welcomed to the brotherhood with open arms, even if those arms were attached to a person who was never entirely sure what Thunder was saying.

Five years later, sitting on the dusty floor of an ancient temple with his friends, wrists bound by some strange kind of rope and surrounded by natives who were not exactly brimming with friendliness, Thunder marveled inwardly at the strange turns his life had taken since that lonely library night in March. Not-Thunder would never have ended up here: that was certain.

Thunder looked over at the others. Falcon was silent, her eyes darting about as she assessed the room and all potential threats. Mano seemed curiously calm, as though he had reached peace with his mortality a long time ago and all of this was old-hat. Kaia had a look on her face Thunder had seen many times, one that usually was followed by a slap to the cheek or a swift kick to the junk. He had a feeling at least one of these guards was going to need some ice on their family pears before the day was over.

Only April seemed outwardly distressed, using what small amount of control over her body she had to chew nervously on her lower lip. Thunder caught her eye and flashed her his trademark grin. She gave a weak smile back, though whether that was because of the effects of the spell or because she was still terrified was hard to tell. Thunder wished he could tell her it was going to be okay. No matter what happened, it would turn out all good, because Thunder had a plan. It didn't involve anything as complicated as Falcon was likely hatching, nor did it center on any contingence of events that would create an opening.

Thunder's plan was simple: when the time came, he would act. It was the same plan he used for every hurdle he faced in his life, and it hadn't let him down yet.

19.

"That was certainly informative," Lawrence said, levitating out of the hole and back onto the stone floor. "I had no idea such enormously powerful beings existed."

"*You know me, always glad to help. Maybe after this I can give you a nice rim job while I fan you with a palm leaf.*"

"I would very much like to express how not on board with that I am," Clint said on Kodi's heels. "Especially since I think my body would be the one he used."

"Relax, I understand your... passenger doesn't speak for you. Once I've finished my work, I'll pluck him out of your head and stick him back in some plant, just to show there are no hard feelings."

"You'd do that?"

"Of course. I'm not a monster. I simply saw an opportunity for tremendous gain and decided to seize it," Lawrence explained. "I did what anyone would do in my situation. Assuming they had the brains and tenacity to pull it off, obviously. I'll be back to free you from your mind parasite soon." Lawrence walked calmly out of the room, leaving Clint still unable to move from the neck down.

He's lying.

"Really? And here I thought the guy holding us all hostage was a respectable gentleman."

No need to get snippy.

"I'm not. You are, and it's bleeding over," Clint sighed. "I thought you were going to stop him from finding what he wanted in my head."

That was the plan, up until he mentioned he would kill everyone if I messed up his brain.

"Right. Probably a good call on that one."

Thought you'd approve. On the plus side, he was so busy rooting around that he didn't notice me doing some snooping of my own. I know what he's doing now.

"You do? That's great! What is it and how do we stop him?"

He's trying to steal my divinity, and we don't.

"We don't?"

The guy has us completely beaten. He's trapped Felbren in a pearl, which is how he's controlling everyone. When he calls Nature using the pear, he'll pretend he's the emissary. She'll sense Felbren's divine power and think it's me, so she'll channel my power to him. Without me there to flow into, it will be stuck inside him, where he'll be able to take control of it.

"Can't Nature see through his trick?"

She could if she gave a crap. To her, this is just a minor annoyance to be done and forgotten about. Hell, she probably doesn't even remember trapping me. That's why the energy in the pear is so important. It's like a dog whistle, except made specifically to summon her for this task.

"Gotcha." Clint dearly wished he could sit down; his legs were getting stiff from holding the slightly hunched position Lawrence had left him in. "Is there anything else?"

Yeah. He's going to kill us all when he's done.

"What?!" Clint's voice echoed across the stone chamber, bouncing down the hallway to ears unknown.

He doesn't want witnesses. He's not trying to start a religion; he's trying to covertly seize power. The only reason we all aren't dead yet is that he's smart enough to save crimes that carry a life in prison for after he no longer has to worry about mortal authorities.

Clint's head swam and for once it wasn't just at frustration from dealing with Kodi. They were going to die. Everyone. Kaia, Mano, Falcon, April, even Thunder. And it was his fault. If he'd just gone to a shrink to talk about the voice in his head instead of going off on some crazy

241

adventure, Lawrence would have never known about gods. They'd all be drinking cocktails made from Kenowai Pears and watching the sun drift below the horizon. Now… now they were probably living their last minutes of life because of Clint.

Hey, are you okay? Things are getting a little… swirly in here.

"Your voice thing. We can use that, can't we? Free ourselves, go off and stop Lawrence?"

I told you: that relies on ambient faith. We're in the temple of one god with another binding us. Even if I could channel enough juice to pop us free without completely shredding you, there's no way we could beat the full power of a god. Not even a half-breed could do that, and those are way stronger than we are right now. For that sort of thing you need direct Belief fueled by one hell of a Want.

"No… no, I don't accept that." Clint's breathing was getting hard; he could swear he was beginning to see spots at the corners of his vision. "There has to be something we can do. Those people are our friends."

Clint… you need to calm down, kid. I can see inside your head and let me tell you, things are beginning to get kind of crazy.

"I don't care." Clint realized his legs had stopped hurting; then he noticed that at some point during his mini freak-out, he'd managed to sit down. He tested his legs and

242

found them still completely immobile. Weird. Very weird. "I don't care about how much power he has. I don't care how hopeless this is. We're going to do something. I will not let him win. He is not going to hurt anyone."

Kid, what the hell is going on with you? This is getting seriously... Oh, shit.

Kodiwandae finally recognized what was happening inside the mind of the mortal where he had set up shop. What had begun as a light blaze of panic had fed upon Clint's fears and guilt, building until it was a roaring inferno tearing through the young man's thoughts. Kodiwandae was seeing something truly miraculous. He was actually witnessing the manifestation of a mortal's first Want. Much like the first Love and the first orgasm, this was going to be a doozy.

It shredded all coherent thought, engulfing every aspect of who Clint was, consuming every memory and dream and hope that comprised what made him Clint until all of him, every last piece, was burning with the same desire:

I Want To Keep Them Safe.

Kodi felt himself growing warm, his attempts to hold it back beginning to falter. It was enveloping him too; he could sense himself being filled by Clint's Want, an unspoken prayer of desperation practically vibrating with need. As the last of his defenses fell and Kodi began to be swept away into the blaze, he felt his own existence expand, filling him with a tingling sensation of power he'd nearly forgotten the flavor of. That was when the jist of his own earlier words came back to him and he realized just how crazy things were about to get: "Mortal's Wants direct and power gods."

Well… This is going to be interesting.

*   *   *

"So bro, what's the policinaltude on last requests?" Thunder asked.

Lawrence stood at the altar, arranging a few final touches for the ceremony. He presumed most of it was formality; however, his careful nature refused to let him skip something that might be important. This was a one-shot opportunity and he refused to see it fail because he'd lit the wrong color of candle. He was momentarily surprised at Thunder's voice; he didn't recall releasing their ability to speak. Perhaps his control weakened as his attention faltered. Something to keep in mind after his ascension.

"Last requests apply to the condemned. I have no intention of killing any of you; I just want to proceed with my business uninterrupted."

If Thunder doubted the man's words, he kept such worries to himself. He'd felt something a few minutes ago,

244

a strange ripple in the force holding him down. Testing had revealed that while his body was still slow to respond, as though he'd beer-bonged a bottle of vodka, it would move under his command. Lawrence's cronies were on the wall, but they hadn't stepped up to guard more closely, so Thunder had a suspicion something had weakened Lawrence's power. If there was going to be action, this was the time.

"Well, then how about letting us get our refreshment on during the shizow? Still a few brewskis in the backpack."

Lawrence resisted the urge to sigh in frustration; it was unbecoming for men such as him. He'd tried to quiet Thunder once more, yet the boy still responded. It was worrying; however, at this point, the most opportune scenario was merely to press ahead in an expedient manner. That meant quieting the boy so Lawrence could think.

"Fine," Lawrence said, walking over and grabbing the satchel. He quickly checked inside, but Thunder was telling the truth. It held nothing more than eight cheap beers, now hot after their lengthy trek. He tossed the bag over and turned back to the altar.

"Thanks, bro. Mind letting us have an arm each as to funkcilitate the drinkage?"

Lawrence smiled inwardly. He'd wondered if more than their mouths had gotten free, but if Thunder was resisting beer then he must still be bound. Knowing that, there was no more reason to play along, but then again, Thunder could be rather annoying when he wanted to be.

"One arm each, and if anyone gets any ideas, I'd like to remind you that you are still surrounded by men with spears."

"Totes," Thunder agreed. After a pause he moved his right arm and grabbed the backpack, unzipping it with his teeth and pulling out a beer. He handed them out, though it involved tossing in some cases where the recipient was too far away. Everyone looked at him with uncertainty; they'd noticed the growing freedom in their appendages as well. He gave them a smile and cracked his beer, then carefully mouthed the words "Not yet."

The others nodded then opened their own beverages. Thunder plucked one more beer from the bag and put in his lap. He wasn't sure what everyone else was going to do when shit got real, but he's already figured out what his best move was.

April found it strange that she was taking her cue from someone like Thunder; then again, he was the only one who'd actually taken any action when he noticed their freedom. Admittedly, it was just getting them beer, but she supposed if she had to witness their demise, it might as well be with a buzz. She didn't believe for a second Lawrence intended to spare them. The man was too rational and that was April's wheelhouse. That and studying. She'd done a lot of reading about Kenowai after learning about their trip. Legends, stories, local agriculture, everything she'd been able to find had been consumed by her brain. Lawrence had likely done the same; he was the type of man to go so far as to learn a new language just to know what the baggage carrier was saying about him. Maybe something he'd found was letting him do all this, which meant if April had read it too then she might be able to stop him. She took another sip of beer and focused the razor-sharp mind that had left her alienated, strange, and academically unstoppable for the majority of her life. This was what she did.

Mano, for his part, was just enjoying the beer. He wondered how his shark friend would be after this crazy white man killed them all. It was too bad; he would have bought the shark a whole case of good dark beer and poured it into the ocean as thanks for his help today. He mentally added a bottle of smooth rum to the list of things to pour. It would end up in the shark's belly, but he could probably still count it as thanks to a god, if he survived. Which god didn't matter so much at the moment; it just seemed unlikely they were getting out of here without someone's help.

Falcon Rainwater had taken a momentary leave of absence; in her place, Valerie Quinn was employing the deductive skills that had made her a terror of a litigator before moving into the world of CEOs. Lawrence wasn't a madman; that would have been a much more preferable scenario. He was simply working off the facts as they were presented before him. Whatever he was doing with the pear would be based on something with the gods, a prospect that would have ruled in lunacy if not for the fact that they were all working under similar beliefs. His movements were

247

graceful and deliberate; the man had received training in his youth and had applied it through his years. Still, there were little giveaways here and there that his age was slowing him: the way he ever so slightly favored his left hip, the one-inch difference in his left shoe that indicated an orthopedic insole, the well-hidden wince when he gripped tightly. He was still a powerful man and could likely have killed them all even without thugs or magic, but he had weaknesses. Valerie had found a few; she kept right on staring, though. She was going to find every last one.

Kaia chugged her beer like an alcoholic coming off a stint at rehab. Everything had gone to hell, nothing was turning out right, and she didn't even know what was real and what was made-up anymore. All she knew was that she was tired of this bullshit: tired of running, tired of being uncertain, tired of not knowing what to do. She'd taken two years of self-defense courses back in New York, and the rule with dealing with male attackers was to go for the balls and the eyes. As soon as the group moved, that was exactly what she intended to do. Kick Lawrence in the balls, get her damn pear, go find Clint, and then see if her friend, Kelokin, back on the island still made his pear moonshine. It wasn't much, but it was a plan, damn it.

"I believe," Lawrence announced. "That it is time to begin."

*   *   *

There is a point in the human mind where all logic, fear, and self-preservation are driven away like demons of failure. It is the place people enter when they do things we consider heroic, things like charging through a hail of bullets to recover a wounded friend, or fighting off a stronger attacker in order to protect people they love. It is one of the few great redeeming qualities of the creature called man. Unfortunately, its use rarely ends well. We prize those examples of success because they are the exception, not the rule.

Most people who decide to win or die almost universally end up doing the latter.

Most people were not currently playing taxi cab to a stranded god.

Clint wasn't sure what had happened, not really. All he knew was that one minute he was bucking against his invisible enclosure with all his might, tormented by the thoughts of his friends being killed, and the next he was free and standing atop the pit. The two guards who had been assigned to watch him were slumped over against the wall, their snores echoing off the stone walls.

"Kodi? I feel kind of strange."

That is probably the least surprising thing anyone has said to me all day.

"It seems like things are sort of… glowing." He glanced down at his skin and realized his mistake. "Oh, never mind. It's just reflecting my glow." That should seem strange, shouldn't it? Why didn't that seem strange?

Focus, kid. We've gone all in on this gamble, so let's make the most of it. We need to find our friends.

"Right." Clint's voice sounded heavy; he ignored it for now. His friends. His friends needed to be free. They needed to be safe. He was going to find them.

He might have said may the gods help Lawrence if they were hurt when he got there, but the gods had already chosen their side. So instead he just hoped it was enough.

*   *   *

"Nature, Constant, I summon you!" Lawrence's voice bounded through the room, the pear in his right hand glowing more intensely with each passing second. His left hand he kept dug into his pocket, a fact that only Falcon/Valerie and April noticed. "I call you here to fulfill your bargain. In the name of Kodiwandae, I summon you!"

"It's considered rude to steal other people's mail."

Lawrence turned to find Clint standing at the entranceway, eyes burning with a golden light that looked suspiciously like the one pouring out of the fruit in Lawrence's hand. His skin rippled with illumination as well, swirling about like candles reflected off a pond. Well... this was unexpected.

There was a clatter of tools crashing to the ground as the guards passed out, collapsing on the spot. Lawrence tried to rouse them, but found a power pushing back from the one coming out of his pearl. So Kodi had found a way to block him. This suspicion was confirmed as the rest of the idiot brigade scrambled to their feet, clearly freed from his binding.

"Get him, Kodi!" Thunder yelled, finishing off his beer in celebration.

"I'm... trying," Clint spat, his words forced out under a weight of stress. For the first time the others noticed how furiously he was sweating and how his legs were beginning to tremble. "He's... strong."

Lawrence smiled. So it seemed this little rally of theirs could only last for so long. That made it easier to deal with. Absentmindedly, he set the pear onto the altar and faced his unchained captives. It was just in time: the tall native woman made a beeline for him, rearing back and delivering a kick that would have put a football through a field goal post from the fifty yard line. He side-stepped easily, resisting the urge to smile as he heard the painful smack of her foot connecting with the stone altar. The island boy was next, flying at him with a clothesline that Lawrence blocked, then replied to with a series of quick punches to the kidney, the pearl still clutched safely in his fist. Mano began coughing and dropped to the ground in pain.

"The left," the old woman screamed. "He's weaker on his left side!"

Had he not been in mid-battle, Lawrence would have been intrigued by her cool-headed assessment. Instead, he was merely impressed. The next one to come at him was Thunder, of all people, charging across the stone floor in a dead sprint.

"Thundeeeeer PUNCH!" The boy dropped the half-empty can in his right hand and pulled it back into a fist. The only way the move could have been more telegraphed was if it had been thrown by Thomas Edison. Lawrence easily dodged the blow and swept Thunder's legs from under him, a subtle cracking sound confirmed he'd taken out one of the attacker's knees. He glanced over to see the remaining risks, two women and a slowly-wilting man under the guidance of a god. Far from the worst odds he'd faced over the years.

"If we're all quite done with this, maybe we can-"

"Thundeeeeer BOMB!" Lawrence whipped back around, expecting Thunder to have crawled back into some kind of attack position. Instead, the young man was still lying prone on the ground, his only movement a rapid shaking of his left hand.

Lawrence figured it out about a second after the pressurized stream of beer struck him in the face. He gagged and coughed as he tried to clear his eyes and breathe past the yeasty concoction. This wasn't helped when he was struck by two soft forms a few seconds later.

The three of them tumbled to the ground, where Thunder and Mano were able to help by grabbing Lawrence and pulling him down. The whole thing dissolved into chaos for a few moments until Lawrence's superior practice and training prevailed. He struck unthinkingly, hitting weak points and causing concussions in rapid succession. It wasn't pretty, but it got him enough time to scramble to his feet away from the crowd.

"That's enough!" Lawrence yelled as he wiped the last of the foam from his face. "I have had my fill of you idiots and your pointless struggling. It is over, you've lost; now face your demise with some sense of propriety and just lay the fuck down!"

"Hey asshole," April said from the ground, her sneer still visible despite the bloody lip she'd gotten in the fray. "Want to know something interesting?"

"No!"

"Too bad." She lifted her hand and held up a small pink sphere. Lawrence knew it in a heartbeat, which was a good thing since his heart skipped the next few that were due.

"You're not the only one with a good memory for details." April reared back and slammed the pearl against the stone floor, obliterating it into dust.

Most pearls do not break quite that easily.

Most pearls do not have a very pissed off god inside.

Lawrence felt an iron grip on his shoulder as he was yanked upward, his feet quickly losing touch with the floor. He twisted around to see Felbren's psychotic grin.

"I think we need to have a talk."

Clint and Kodi smiled together as the god appeared, the weight of their task finally lifted. Clint went to blink his dry eyes and discovered they refused to re-open. He fell to the ground heavily, not even registering the sting of pain at impact as he drifted into unconsciousness.

20.

The rest of the recently-freed pear hunters barely had a chance to register Clint's collapse before his eyes popped open and he jumped back to his feet. There was something different about him, though: his skin seemed darker than before, and though his eyes still glowed, it was like molten gold more than beaming light.

"We have to hurry," Kodi said through Clint's mouth.

"Wait, what just happened to Clint?" Kaia asked, slowly picking herself up and ignoring the toes she was certain were broken.

"He used his own prayers to power my divine abilities, then channeled them through himself. Mortal souls aren't built to handle that kind of energy."

"So… is he okay?" The fact that Thunder asked such a question in normal words drove home the seriousness of the situation to the others even more than Kodi's own explanation had.

"I have no idea, but I know the sooner I'm out of him, the better his chances." Kodi strode across the room, pausing only briefly to speak with Felbren. *"I trust we're past the point of petty interference?"*

"The boy helped to free me and kept this one from joining our divine ranks. My debt to him outweighs any of our squabbles."

"Good." He finished crossing the room and grabbed the pear from the altar. There was a tingle that surged up Clint's fingers as they grasped the glowing fruit, a sensation akin to completing a circuit. Kodi hoped it wasn't doing more damage, but at this point, he was pretty much out of options.

"Nature! Hurry your ass up and get down here! My name is Kodiwandae, god of Kenowai, former prisoner of your own stupid machinations, and currently passenger in this mor- my friend, Clint. Now uphold our bargain and come set me FREE!"

"No need to yell. I've been here since the scheming old man called."

Everyone turned to the back of the room where a new figure had appeared. No, that wasn't quite right. It hadn't simply appeared. It was telling the truth; now that they thought back, it had been there since Lawrence set down the pear. Somehow their brains had simply been unable to grasp what their eyes tried to tell them.

It was a she, or at least it had chosen to look like one, a woman with hair that started off green, then turned yellow, then orange, and then brown before ceasing to be. Her skin was the color of chestnut and cherry blossoms, and if you think those are very different colors, then just

256

imagine how confused the people looking at her felt. She was beautiful, but in the way one might admire a well-forged blade: aesthetics undeniably tinted with a sense of danger. Her simple brown dress dragged the floor, small plants rising whenever it trailed.

Everyone felt reasonably comfortable assuming this was who Kodi had been trying to call.

"Why didn't you... never mind. I won't like the answer and right now it doesn't matter. Hurry up and get me out."

"In such a hurry to be free. Well, I suppose you have been stuck a long while." Suddenly she wasn't in the back of the room, she was next to Clint, who seemed quite unsurprised at the spontaneous teleportation. *"Or is it some other reason? Tell me, Kodiwandae, have you taken to caring for this vessel of yours?"*

"This vessel has a name. All of these mortals do. And yes, I do care for them. They showed me kindness and aid when they owed me nothing."

"You are a god. Is it not their place to serve you?"

Clint's eyes sparked, literally throwing off a small shower of light. *"I am not here to debate our role in the world or the basis of the symbiotic relationship between mortal and god. I am here to complete our ritual and get the hell out of Clint before I do any more damage."*

"Caring for individual mortals is a dangerous road, Kodiwandae. It has been the path of destruction for many of our kind before you, but it has also been the path to greatness for a few. And you have the seeds of greatness within you. I should know; after all, seeds are something of my specialty."

Her hand settled on Clint's forehead, long fingers enveloping the entire span of his cranium. A wind blew through the temple, carrying the scent of an impending storm. Those who had been at the tree where this all began felt a sense of déjà vu.

"Very well. Let us finish this."

*   *   *

Clint's eyes fluttered open to reveal a world of swirling colors, a lazy kindergartener's attempt at art. For a moment he feared his vision had been destroyed; however, after a few blinks he realized he was merely coming out of an extremely deep sleep. The world cleared to reveal a circle of people standing over him, concern apparent on all their faces. It was all of his friends, plus a face that he didn't know but that somehow looked incredibly familiar.

258

"Kodiwandae, I assume?"

The stranger gave him a dazzling a smile, white teeth accentuated all the more by his tan skin. *"In the flesh. Finally."*

More hands than he could count reached down and pulled him to his feet, each taking as much care as was possible. His head went dizzy for a moment, then things righted themselves and he was able to stand under his own power.

"How do you feel?"

How did he feel? Different: no question there. The sensation he'd gotten after using just a word of Kodi's power paled in comparison to this. He didn't think he'd ever be quite the same again. Then again, that wasn't necessarily a bad thing. People changed all the time. They had experiences, they grew, they became new versions of themselves: sometimes for the better, sometimes for the worse. He was not the same Clint who had first come to the island; however, he doubted he was looking at the same April, or Falcon, or Kaia, or Mano, or... well, maybe the same Thunder. But probably not the same Kodiwandae as had been sealed away so many years ago. He was different. Maybe that was okay.

"I feel better than I did in the pit, I'll tell you that."

Kodi laughed and it wasn't long before the others were joining in. It wasn't all that funny; it was just a sense

259

of relief that after coming so close to the edge, it was beginning to seem like they were going to be all right.

"*That makes me happier than I can tell you,*" Kodi said. "*I owe you, all of you, a tremendous debt. As does my friend, Felbren.*"

Clint noticed for the first time that there were other people in the room that were not crowded around him. Felbren was there, still holding Lawrence, who seemed to have been magically silenced, at least given how furiously he was shouting without producing words. Nature stood beside him, a gentle smile on her face and a faint glimmer of boredom in her eyes. He didn't take it personally; to her, this probably was not even a blip on the radar.

"Still a friend?"

"*I know this might be hard to understand, but in our world, the extent of his actions amount to little more than a practical joke, like putting a bucket of water on a slightly open door for your friend to walk through.*"

"Really?"

"*No, but I don't have the heart to abandon him. I'm the only real friend he still has.*"

"You're a solid bro, Kodi," Thunder chimed in.

"*As are all of you, solid bros.*"

The mortal group exchanged a look, debating the idea of correcting Kodi before such terms sank into his vocabulary; however, he continued speaking before they got a chance. *"I'm afraid we need to be going soon. I've been absent of my island for too long, and there are other matters to attend to as well. I wanted you to know that you all have my thanks, though, and as that you all carry my divine blessing."*

"What does that mean?" April, always the stickler, asked.

"I am not a world-renowned god, but I do hold some power. From now on, I will hear your prayers above all others. Additionally, pears will now hold minor healing properties for you. It will not regrow a leg; however, small cuts and headaches are a thing of the past for you."

"Does the brew-ju work on hangovers?" Thunder asked.

"Of course."

"Aw man, but then I'd have to chompers down a pear. Yucksville. Lady or the tiger, bro."

"We thank you, oh generous one," Falcon butted in. "What will become of Lawrence, though?"

"There is a special punishment for those who try to steal from the gods. I assure you, he will not trouble any of you in the future." They might have wanted more details,

but the gleam in Felbren's eyes stayed their tongues. Sometimes it was easier to sleep at night not knowing certain things.

Nature cleared her throat, which resulted in three plants turning brown and dying, reminding Kodiwandae that there was only so much time for goodbyes.

"We must be off. Thank you again, my friends. We've arranged for Lawrence's boat to return you to Kenowai where you can catch your plane. If you need any assistance on the way, well, I'll be listening."

Kodi started to turn away, however he turned back and stuck out his hand to Clint. The mortal seized the divine appendage and the two shook; however, before it was over, Kodi pulled Clint in close and whispered to him, *"I do not know what lies in store for you. Never has a mortal done what you did, so there is no precedent to work from. Just know that, whatever happens, you have friends in high places you can turn to."* Then their embrace was broken and Kodiwandae stood with the other gods.

There was no pomp or showmanship. One minute they were standing, Kodiwandae waving, Nature looking away, Felbren sulking, and Lawrence screaming bloody murder with nary a sound produced, and then they were all simply gone.

"Awesomsauce," Thunder said, the others quietly echoing his sentiment. The group began heading out of the temple, too exhausted to engage in discussion after all they'd been through.

Since the hallway out was narrow, Clint found himself walking next to Kaia, who greeted his presence with a warm smile. They locked eyes for a moment then Clint grew nervous and turned his away. That was strange; he didn't usually get nervous about anything.

"Clint," Kaia said, her voice strange. "What color are your eyes?"

"Just brown."

"That's what I thought. Nothing special about them, right?"

"Nope. Dull, boring, brown, that's me."

She reached into her reclaimed purse and fiddled around for a bit, eventually pulling out a compact mirror. Wordlessly, she opened it and handed it to Clint. He stopped walking to take a look, though at first he wasn't sure what she wanted him to see. Then it was clear. He wondered how he'd missed it.

Gold. Undeniable flecks of gold were scattered across the dull brown canvas of his irises. When he tilted his head they seemed to shimmer, never quite in the same place any two times that he looked. Who knows how long he would have stood there admiring himself if Kaia's voice hadn't broken the spell.

"So, what do you think it means?"

21.

Edward Dillon emerged from his private elevator to find a small army of men in suits milling around his office, one woman in similar dress at the center. She was seated at his desk, a pile of folders set before her and a cheap romance novel in her hands. She glanced up at his entrance then stuck a bookmark in the pages, momentarily halting Rodrigo's romantic advances on the widow Tilston.

"Good morning, Mr. Dillon."

"Miss… Rainwater, wasn't it? I didn't get word that you'd all returned from the island yet."

"Yes, unfortunately all of your lackeys are in various forms of custody for the crimes they committed during our trip. I only paused long enough to pop by my old office and gather up a few supplies before coming to see you. Please, have a seat."

"You're in my chair," Edward Dillon pointed out, hoping she would vacate without making him call security. Hurling a woman with grey hair out into the streets would be terrible publicity.

"Actually, I'm not. Why don't you sit down and let me explain? If you'd like, I'll even send the goon-squad out the door."

He weighed his options. None of the men looked terribly imposing, but the lady lecturing him from the chair seemed to control them effortlessly. She was blocking his emergency button under the desk; he could call from his phone if he kept her distracted, though. With a seemingly innocuous shrug he set his coffee down and plopped into one of his visitor chairs. Obeying some unseen cue, the men in suits all walked out his office door, shutting it firmly behind them.

"Mr. Dillon, I would like to tell you a story."

"If this is about your money, there is a two-week mailing period from our central accounting office. This is not the appropriate way to look for expedition."

"It is a story of a young, ambitious woman named Valerie Quinn," she continued, verbally plowing right over him. "She was a smart girl, and hungry. She came from a poor family, so she worked herself to the bone academically. Valerie managed to get admission into a top-tier law school, later passing the bar on her first try. After that, she started working on business law while also earning her MBA. Her formidable intellect, education, and personality led the people who faced her to start calling her Valerie the Valkyrie. They meant it as an insult, but she took it as a complement. Eventually, Valerie moved up in the world, crushing more beneath her as she started her own consulting firm while chairing the boards of several other Fortune 500 corporations. Then, one day, about twelve years ago, Valerie met an enemy she couldn't beat back. Do you know what that was?"

"The boredom of the people she was talking to?"

"Cancer. Not for her, that would have been too just. No, it came for her younger sister, a dear girl named Melissa, who had raised three fine children and worked with some local charities in her free time. Valerie spared no expense in her treatment, but even her impressive wealth wasn't enough to help Melissa. In Valerie's darkest hour, sitting in the hospital chapel, waiting for the inevitable to happen, she did something she had long ago dismissed as lunacy. Valerie prayed. She'd never been big on the organizational deities; however, the idea of nature having a collective consciousness had appealed to her. So she made Mother Earth an offer: if Melissa could be spared then Valerie would change her ways. No more aggressive tactics, no more worship of the almighty dollar. She would give up meat, she would do all she could to live in harmony with her surroundings. Valerie would trade away everything she knew if only she could keep her sister."

"Let me guess: your sister lived and that's why you showed up to my office going by Falcon and dressed like a hippie?" Edward Dillon checked his watch. "If we're done, I really do have to get to work. There are several important meetings scheduled for today."

"All you have on your calendar is a golf game and two hours set aside to tool with your fantasy football lineup," she corrected. Edward was a professional, so he did not blush in embarrassment at being called out. His hands did tighten on his coffee mug, however.

267

"You're right, she made a miraculous recovery. Still alive today, over in Colorado. And I kept my deal, because I'm a businesswoman. Thanks to you, though, I had an interesting experience over the past week, and I got to meet the very incarnation of what I prayed to that day."

"I beg your pardon?"

"It would take too long to explain, and you wouldn't believe me anyway. Suffice it to say that while one of my friends was unconscious I had some free time, so I spoke to Nature in the flesh, and thanked her personally for saving my sister. Know what she said?"

"Given the turn the conversation has taken, I'd wager it to be something crazy."

"She had no idea what I was talking about. It might have been divine intervention that saved Melissa, or just the drugs finally working. Either way, it wasn't the work of the deity I made my bargain with, which means I am no longer bound by those granola-eating practices. Though I'll say that my time as Falcon was not entirely wasteful. I learned a lot about myself, and about how to be a kinder, more loving person. Now, let's get to the meat of the matter. I'm taking over your company."

"My, you really have gone down the path of madness, haven't you?" Edward hit send on the phone he'd been covertly dialing under the chair. Now it was just a matter of time.

"Possibly, but too bad for you I'm still excellent at what I do." Valerie slid the first folder over to him. "This will detail how I bought up most of your board's share this morning through lucrative offers they would have been fools to pass up." She slid him the next one. "This will show how Lawrence Farran, who owned a sizable stake in your company, transferred those shares over to me before his incarceration. Feel free to challenge them, though I don't think you'll have much luck."

Edward reviewed the documents with a growing sense of dread. She hadn't quite managed to get majority control with her antics, but she was close. Much closer than he was comfortable with.

"Good effort, but you're short."

"Ah, but I still have a folder left." She slid the last one over, a jungle cat's smile dancing on her face. "That one, as you will read, deals with the shares belonging to your son, who we know as Thunder. Seems you've been giving him some every year as a birthday gift since he was born. Well, at least up until four years ago. Still, it was enough to give me majority."

Edwards felt his coffee twist uncomfortably in his stomach.

"He's a loyal son, would only sell me what I needed under very specific terms. You'll stay on in a leadership role, though I will be looking over your shoulder to make certain we don't have any cultural boondoggles like the one you pulled in Kenowai. Every one of the contest winners is still paid their prize money, checks due out this afternoon. I am not allowed to make any large scale cut-backs to the company, nor can I gut it for its recipes and distributors then leave it to wither on the vine. There are a few other caveats, but the long and short is that the company is protected. I must say, he has a surprisingly extensive grasp of business practices."

"He used to be such a smart boy."

"He still is," the new head of Camelot Burgers replied. "I think perhaps you just don't understand his particular brand of wisdom. Don't worry; you'll have ample time to let it grow on you as you work together."

"Work together?" By this point it was all Edward could do to string two words together.

"Certainly. You'll be teaching him the business starting next year. Neither of us is getting younger, and I think it's time we started looking ahead to the future of our company. Besides, he was adamant on the idea of wanting to spend more time with his father."

Edward Dillon was dimly aware of the sound of opening doors as the men in suits flooded back into the office. Security was with them; however, he had a sinking suspicion they weren't here to come to his rescue.

"That will be all, Edward. Security will help you move to your new cubicle ten floors down. I think it's high

270

time you started getting to know the cogs that keep this company running."

*   *   *

Mano finished pouring the golden-brown liquid into the ocean, watching it dissipate slowly amidst the crashing waves. The empty rum bottle went into the same wagon he'd used to haul the case of beer, now only empty cans. Mano was also a person who kept his bargains, though at the moment he wasn't sure who to dedicate such an offering to. It seemed like he was on good terms with Kodiwandae and Felbren, and he wasn't all that certain the goddess of Denilale gave a crap about this sort of thing, so he decided that it was for the sea god, Iohalo.

He asked that the ruler of the waves watch over his shark friend and grant safe passage to all the sea travelers that came to Kenowai with goodness in their hearts. If they came to conquer, he could let them drown, though it probably wouldn't make a whole lot of difference. Kenowai was no longer the land of the absentee god.

The wagon groaned in protest as Mano trucked it down the cliff, pausing only to throw some Kenowai Pears into it along with the empty rum bottle and beer cans. He'd tried a few since getting home and their flavor had somehow become more exceptional against his tongue. They'd worked their way back into his diet in greater

271

number since before he'd first grown sick of them as a child. Mostly it was because they now tasted so delicious.

Good health was important too, though. Especially when one lived on an island like this one.

*　　　*　　　*

If April had been the kind of person who had friends, they would have seen the subtle change in her when she returned to school. Then again, if April had been the kind of person who had friends, she wouldn't have needed the change as badly in the first place. To their credit, her colleagues did notice something about her as she walked the pristine halls of academia. It wasn't the way her mouth now occasionally pulled into a smile, or that her eyes had a hint of laughter in them that had been absent before. It wasn't even that she was looking around and seeing people's faces rather than keeping her head crammed into a book. In fairness, those were subtle differences, and what drew their attention was a much larger one.

"Dudette, that psychology department is like huzaaaaaaah bigguns."

"More space than they need for a soft science," April replied, taking Thunder's arm and guiding him away to the next stop on the campus tour.

"Nah way! Psychology is the mark of our greatness as a species. To seek outward mysteries is natural; to seek understanding of what lies within ourselves is courageous."

April blinked. "Wait, what?"

"Nothing, bro, don't worry about it. Oh shit! Look at that librizzle!" He rushed off toward the library, enraptured at every new sight around him. She didn't think she'd ever get accustomed to his bouts of intelligence, or his strange way of speaking, or his mysterious way of being positive about everything. At least, she hoped not.

No one had more been surprised than she when Thunder asked if he could come see her college. No one had been more surprised than Thunder when she said yes. It was a terrible match by all measurable standards. She couldn't really picture who would make a good fit for Thunder; then again, she couldn't picture a good fit for herself either. She used to be able to: a solid man with a robust intellect who shared her need for absolute silence when studying. Now, no matter how she tried, she just couldn't. Something was different, and that ideal man wasn't so ideal anymore. Many months would pass before April would acknowledge that what had changed was her.

There are moments in life, great moments that reach us down in our core, moments that change us in ways we can never come back from. They do not come with invitations or announcements. They can only be truly recognized and appreciated when looking back in retrospect. April had just finished living her great moment. Others are undoubtedly living theirs right now.

"Yo, April, you need a Thunder-back ride?" He'd gotten a ways ahead, but had slowed down to wait as she caught up. This was a terrible idea and a match-up that went in the face of all discernible logic.

Still... it wasn't boring. And for some reason, that mattered now.

"Like you can keep up!" April yelled, pumping her legs into a sprint and racing past him toward the library. Who got there first is irrelevant in the telling.

Both of them were the winners.

*   *   *

Kaia looked into her suitcase uncertainly. Five pears, a sweater, a jacket, pants, shorts, a tank-top, a t-shirt, shoes, heels, boots, a toothbrush, underwear, and a swimsuit. This was the problem with being a world-trotting adventurer: never knowing what was appropriate to pack. Sure, she was only starting off by heading to America, but who knew what came after that? Kaia Hale was something that had quite possibly never existed before: an academic who Believed. The path before her was uncharted, to say the least. There were so many legends in the world, so many stories to investigate.

She took out one of her t-shirts and added a long-sleeve turtleneck. She was more susceptible to cold than heat, after all. Kenowai had given her the gift of perspective and it was hard to find a place hotter than she would remember this place being. There were candidates, sure; maybe she'd feel the sting of the sun while in Egypt searching for Anubis, or in the deserts of Arizona trying to make contact with one of the Native American spirit gods. She added another swimsuit, this one a bit skimpier than her first. If memory served, Coyote was a god who liked his women to show more flesh than less.

Besides, she at least knew her first stop on the tour, and she was pretty certain she could drag Clint to one of Pensacola's many beaches. Just because he was likely to end up the thesis of her research didn't mean she couldn't enjoy their time together. It might not be strictly within research protocol, but then again, neither was carrying pears as a substitute for a first aid kit.

Research protocol could suck it. Kaia was creating her own standards now.

*   *   *

The shark greedily swam through Mano's offering, allowing the liquor to course across its gills. Now this was what he was talking about! Dark beer and a stout chaser; that island boy could sure show some gratitude. The shark would make a special point of watching over his surfing activities for the next few months. No great white assclownfish was going to gobble down this hammerhead's drink ticket.

Something pulled against the shark's rough skin for a minute, a brine shrimp tumbling about in the current. If the shrimp seemed somehow familiar to the shark, as though perhaps it had once been a predator as well, such similarities went unnoticed. As did the soft, almost inaudible, scream that somehow emanated from the shrimp's mouth. It was gone in seconds anyway, pulled away into the greater ocean at large, where creatures would find it appetizing rather than annoying. Even if the shark had heard, it wouldn't have made a difference. The hammerhead didn't speak English.

It merely spoke the universal language of friendship over a shared drink.

*   *   *

There are many legends of the Return of Kodiwandae. Some include the story of the mortals who assisted him, though as time wore on, more and more versions turned his helpers to natives rather than foreigners. All versions, curiously enough, include the King of Kenowai, who helped deliver the god back to his people. The tales disagree on whether Kodiwandae returned first to his island to look upon his people or whether he went straight to Alendola to see Alahai and confess his love at last.

No version debates that the reception Kodiwandae received from the goddess was any less than earth-shaking, due in no small part to the minor earthquake which came two days after he gained his freedom. The two found deep love within one another, so firm and powerful that over time even Felbren's jealousy was eventually softened and his friendship with Kodiwandae renewed. What followed in their relationship is also the stuff of legends, though those must wait for another day. This is only the tale of how Kodiwandae gained his freedom.

That said, there is one small detail that none of the legends include. It is not the storytellers' fault, for how could they tell what even the gods were unaware of?

It is a small matter, but when the gods vanished from Denilale, they went to different places. Felbren was sent to his island with the mortal in his grip. Kodiwandae meant to go to Alendola; however, he wound up in Kenowai by mistake (this is where the confusion in the tales comes from). Nature, on the other hand, went exactly where she meant to go. She went to a small field on Alendola, miles from the city and with a beautiful view of the ocean. Wildflowers grew throughout the grass, and many shrines to Alahai had been erected over the millennia she had been worshipped. Nature's form grew soft and malleable, reshaping into that of a younger woman who seemed of the same race as Kodiwandae and Felbren. She wore nothing more than a white toga, her long hair swept up in the breeze that had suddenly found itself compelled to blow.

The woman who had been Nature and was now Alahai looked at the beautiful colors of the sunset reflecting off the waves. Kodiwandae would be here soon; she'd only sent him to his island so she had time to change. It was a woman's prerogative to look her best when meeting her lover, after all. Perhaps one day she would explain to him that Alahai was the form this Constant took when it wished to unwind, and that she had neither meant to seduce him nor to fall in love herself, but that day would not be today. The pain of his incarceration was likely still too fresh. Today was about happiness.

It would be a good day, too. Kodiwandae was a wonderful being: his only flaw was his fear of action. Alahai had great confidence that would no longer be an issue, not after the adventure she'd given him. Of course, she underestimated the size of the adventure she was embarking on herself.

But that was a lover's prerogative as well.

*   *   *

Clint absentmindedly played with a laser-pointer as he stared at the clock. The King of Kenowai darted about the room, intent on catching the red dot that eluded him. Clint had expected some resistance from the staff when the island cat had followed him home; however, no one had remarked as it sauntered royally down the halls, always a few steps behind him. He'd probably need to go get a litter box and some actual cat toys: something about the laser-pointer felt mean-spirited. It was all he had for the moment, though, and the King of Kenowai didn't seem to mind, so he continued zipping it about while the hands on the clock counted closer to the start of the day.

Not much longer now: the scent of Mr. Timmons' nitro coffee filled the retirement community, waking all who dared try to sleep past the moment when it was brewed. Rose would be wheeling out the people who were having a bit of trouble getting around. They'd be in the TV lounge bright and early. Today was the day the man from the evaluation committee came to make sure they still qualified for Golden Acres. Rose would get Mrs. Adams first, situate her in the middle of the room so by the time the others were in place and the man got to her, he'd be just balanced between eager to start and ready to be done. The pinnacle of boredom was the spot where some cases could slip through. Even that wouldn't be enough for Mrs. Adams, not the way she was now.

Clint pulled the apple pie from the freezer - the fridge wouldn't have kept it fresh for the length of time he was away - and popped it into the microwave. He set down the laser pointer as he watched the small calorie-laden treat spin in radiation circles, forgetting to turn it off and leaving the red dot resting three feet off the ground on the far wall. A few seconds later there was a small crunching noise that was overshadowed by the microwave's ding of completion.

Clint slid the steaming pastry onto a paper plate, then went to the refrigerator and pulled out two pears from the dozen he'd purchased after getting in last night. Balancing the three items as he opened the door wasn't the easiest task, but he managed it without any serious issues.

Glancing back, he noticed the cat chewing on something. It was hard to make out among the rapid movements of its teeth, but he could swear he caught a flash of red light every now and then. It wouldn't be until later that he discovered the laser pointer was unable to create a dot any longer, regardless of how many times he changed the batteries.

"Your majesty," Clint said, calling to his companion. Sprinkles rose from his devouring, gave a final gulp, and trotted into the hallway. It had not been an easy decision, leaving his island to follow this young man back to his home. It had weighed greatly on the conscience of Sprinkles before his choice was made. Ultimately, the return of Kodiwandae had been the tipping point in deciding whether to immediately return or not. The god needed time to settle in, re-acclimate. He and Sprinkles could come to terms on whose authority superseded whose once there had been adequate time for rejoicing and rest. Until then, Sprinkles was going to stick near the thing he found curious. Though a godling and a king, Sprinkles was, after all, also a cat.

"Good morning, Mrs. Adams." Clint set the apple pie, now cooled off from liquid lava to merely scalding, on the breakfast tray in front of her. He also deposited one of

280

his pears. The other he slipped into his jacket pocket. Mrs. Adams looked up at him with vacant eyes; not even the faint glimmer he'd imagined a week ago remained.

He hunkered down into a squatting position. There were plenty of available seats; however, he didn't intend to stay for long.

"I know you're having trouble remembering who I am, and that's okay for right now. You've had a long, very bad dream for the last six months. I've got good news for you, though. It's morning. Mr. Timmons is making coffee, Rose is bringing you eggs, and I've saved an apple pie from Camelot Burger for you. Morning is here, Mrs. Adams. It is time to **wake up**."

The old woman's eyes widened at his last two words, rousing from their half-closed state to one that seemed to resemble alertness. Clint smiled at her and pulled himself to his feet. "You have a great day, Mrs. Adams. We'll talk when I get back tonight." He headed off toward the exit, the cat walking a few paces behind him.

Such a nice young man. Mrs. Adams realized she hadn't thanked him for the apple pie. Her wrinkled finger ran along its surface, judging the internal heat. Too hot to eat without getting burned, but close to perfect. To kill time, she took a bite of the pear Clint had also left with her. She didn't recall being a fan of them before, but this one was downright scrumptious. Her head cleared with each bite, and by the end, she realized some jackass had left the Spanish soap opera channel on. Why in the hell hadn't she changed that? Grabbing the remote, she turned on a replaying of last night's monster truck rally. Much more like it. Now where was Rose with breakfast? For that matter, why was she sitting here instead of slipping tobacco into the doctor's coffee? So much to do and so little time. Why on earth had she just been sitting around? Mrs. Adams couldn't quite recall, but in the end it didn't matter. She wasn't one to dwell on what had been; her passion lay in plunging forward.

Clint made it outside just as it was beginning to drizzle. There was an umbrella stand by the front of the foyer where a communal collection had formed as people brought in new ones and owners of old ones left Golden Acres. He selected a long grey one with a flat cane handle. Sprinkles pulled closer to him as they stepped outside. The cat disliked any moisture greater than a single tongue could administer. Being nearer to Clint filled Sprinkles' nose with the scents and the sense of the young man; a mortal who was not a god, yet had been seared too greatly by divine energies to be called a human. No half-breed, relying on ambient faith like those of Sprinkles' ilk. Clint was something unseen before in this world. A mortal whose divine power came solely from his own Wants. Such a thing was dangerous, and strange, and curious. Sprinkles and Mrs. Adams had much in common, the first on the list being that they were both greatly looking forward to what lay ahead of them.

"Stay close, I don't think you want to fall into a puddle," Clint cautioned. His hand reflexively dug into his pocket and brushed against the pear inside. It had a good weight, one that reminded him of all the memories he now carried with him, as well as the responsibilities. The hand emerged with a cough drop, which Clint promptly popped in his mouth. Using The Voice still left him with a sore throat, though it was a small price to pay.

"Let's get going. There's a lot of work to do."

About the Author

Drew Hayes is an aspiring author from Texas who has now found time and gumption to publish a few books (so far). He graduated from Texas Tech with a B.A. in English, because evidently he's not familiar with what the term "employable" means. Drew has been called one of the most profound, prolific, and talented authors of his generation, but a table full of drunks will say almost anything when offered a round of free shots. Drew feels kind of like a D-bag writing about himself in the third person like this. He does appreciate that you're still reading, though.

Drew would like to sit down and have a beer with you. Or a cocktail. He's not here to judge your preferences. Drew is terrible at being serious, and has no real idea what a snippet biography is meant to convey anyway. Drew thinks you are awesome just the way you are. That part, he meant. You can reach Drew with questions or movie offers at NovelistDrew@gmail.com Drew is off to go high-five random people, because who doesn't love a good high-five? No one, that's who.

Made in the USA
Las Vegas, NV
17 August 2022